DATE DUE JUN 0 4

7 - 7			
APR 0 4 2005			
Dirty Edge Noted 9/13/04			
GAYLORD			PRINTED IN U.S.A.

Long Way Home

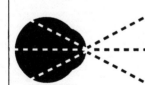 This Large Print Book carries the
Seal of Approval of N.A.V.H.

Long Way Home

Gena Dalton

Thorndike Press • Waterville, Maine

Published in 2004 by arrangement with
Harlequin Books S.A.

Thorndike Press® Large Print Christian Romance.

The tree indicium is a trademark of Thorndike Press.

The text of this Large Print edition is unabridged.
Other aspects of the book may vary from the original edition.

Set in 16 pt. Plantin by Al Chase.

Printed in the United States on permanent paper.

ISBN 0-7862-6371-7 (lg. print : hc : alk. paper)

This book is for my friends,
Jill and Sheila

As the Founder/CEO of NAVH, the only national health agency solely devoted to those who, although not totally blind, have an eye disease which could lead to serious visual impairment, I am pleased to recognize Thorndike Press* as one of the leading publishers in the large print field.

Founded in 1954 in San Francisco to prepare large print textbooks for partially seeing children, NAVH became the pioneer and standard setting agency in the preparation of large type.

Today, those publishers who meet our standards carry the prestigious "Seal of Approval" indicating high quality large print. We are delighted that Thorndike Press is one of the publishers whose titles meet these standards. We are also pleased to recognize the significant contribution Thorndike Press is making in this important and growing field.

Lorraine H. Marchi, L.H.D.
Founder/CEO
NAVH

* Thorndike Press encompasses the following imprints: Thorndike, Wheeler, Walker and Large Print Press.

But it was only right we should celebrate and rejoice, because your brother here was dead and has come to life; he was lost and is found.

— *Luke* 15:32

Chapter One

For maybe half of his ride on the brindle bull, Monte McMahan believed.

That he could stay on for the whole eight seconds.

That he could score high enough to put him back in the running.

That his injured back had healed enough to let him keep going on down the rodeo road.

Then the wily old Brahma dropped his head, shook his ugly horns and spun hard to the right when he'd definitely been looking to the left ever since the first jump out of the chute.

Pain clamped on to Monte's spine like a coyote's teeth around a rabbit. It twisted the breath out of his lungs one second before it sucked the strength from his arms and legs and tore the rigging from his hand.

He flew through space with the bright lights sparkling and the dust shimmering across his vision. He couldn't close his eyes. He would not. If he closed his eyes, he'd be giving up and if he gave up, he'd be dead when he hit the ground.

The impact made him believe he was. But then the pain exploded inside his head and took the place of his last gasp of precious air. He decided a man could live without breathing because a dead man wouldn't be hurting.

A dead man wouldn't be hearing the true concern in the announcer's voice. Good old Butch, he was worried about Monte.

"Folks, put your hands together for Monte McMahan," he boomed. "He's one tough Texas bull rider and he's been ridin' through the pain for a lot of months now. Y'all may've just had the privilege of seeing his last ride, right here in Houston to-night."

The applause started, but it didn't grow. It was hesitant, it died and the fear-filled hush fell over the arena again.

"He's not moved a muscle since he hit," Butch said. "Let's hope Old Brindle hasn't sent him back to the Rocking M for good. As you all know, Monte's one of the fourth or fifth generation of McMahans from that famous ranch in the Hill Country."

Good old Butch needed to get another line of patter. It was nobody's business where Monte was from.

10

Faces, blurry and worried, bent over Monte.

"Boys, get that ambulance on out here," Butch called. "And we need a big thank-you, friends and neighbors, for our brave bullfighting clowns. They've got Old Brindle outta here, now. There he is, joggin' down the run, already lookin' for his next victim."

Monte cringed inside, in spite of the fact he couldn't move a muscle. *Victim.* Butch coulda talked all night without calling him that.

Fool, maybe. That'd be more like it. And now he was a crippled fool.

No, he was not. He would not be.

Calling on the raw willpower that had carried him through many a scrape, he tried once, twice, then he caught his breath and he could force his arm to move. He lifted his hand. He waved to the crowd. Their noise returned, instantly surged into a roar.

He would come back. It might take him a little while, but he'd come back.

All the time the guys from the sports medicine trailer worked on him and examined him and then clamped the stabilizer around his neck and slid him onto the backboard, he held that thought.

Jo Lena Speirs sat her horse on top of the

11

hill and let him blow. She loved this spot overlooking the entrance to the Rocking M. The river bridge glinted in the dying sunlight, far up the narrow highway, and the bluffs on the other side of it lifted green trees to the sky.

"This is getting to be our routine, isn't it, Scooter?" she said, patting his sweaty neck. "Prayers at the old chapel, and then a nice run across the Rocking M before dark."

Which, to be honest, was what was keeping her sane. Trying to be a mother without a husband, a business owner without employees and a daughter without siblings kept her busy every minute.

She'd already prayed this prayer at the chapel, but she said it again, her heart filled with gratitude.

"Bless Bobbie Ann, Lord. Bless her for offering this horse and this place of peace to me."

An old truck and trailer slowed on the highway and turned off onto the Rocking M road. Idly, she watched it. Dexter Hawkins, Bobbie Ann's old neighbor.

Strangely, Dexter didn't follow the road toward the house. He pulled across the entrance and stopped. He must be having trouble. With a truck that old, anything could be wrong.

Jo Lena touched the cell phone she wore on her belt — Dexter, famous for his stinginess, certainly wouldn't have one. She'd ride down there and offer to call for help.

But as she picked up her reins and started to turn, the passenger door to the truck opened. The instant the man stepped foot on the ground, even though he wore a battered hat pulled down, she knew him.

Monte. Monte McMahan. The only man she'd ever loved.

Even though he was stove up and stiff, she'd have known him by the way he moved. She'd have known him in a dust storm, in the dark or in a blizzard.

She'd have known him by the way her heart left her body.

Her eyes strained toward him painfully through the gathering dusk, hungrily watching him limp toward the back of the trailer. Her whole body had gone weak as water.

But the real trouble was her heart. It was pounding like hoofbeats at a gallop — except that her heart had really leapt out of her chest and left her far behind.

It had wrapped itself around Monte. He looked so sore and so completely defeated that she couldn't stand it. Just the sight of him was breaking her apart all over again.

13

Dear Lord, You're going to have to help me now. Please, please, help me remember everything Monte did wrong.

He had done her mightily wrong and she had done everything right. Her mind knew that. But there went her heart, anyway, welcoming him home as if her choice had been wrong and his had been right.

Yes. There went her heart.

And then, when he painfully held on to the trailer and pushed himself up onto the fender so he could crawl onto the horse, he wrenched her very soul. He took her hard-won peace that had been six years in the making.

It wasn't just that he was physically hurt. Or that it killed her to see the hopeless set to his shoulders.

It was simply that he was Monte and she loved him.

She'd thought the fire was long since cold, but there were embers hidden in the ashes. She still loved him.

Dear Lord, give me strength. With Your help, I can handle that. What I can't handle is getting involved with him again.

But that, too, was a forlorn hope. At that instant she recognized the horse he was riding at that painfully slow walk.

The mare was heavier — maybe pregnant

— and scruffier, but she knew her, too, by the way she moved. It was Quick Way Annie, favorite friend of her childhood. The horse she'd been trying to find.

Her mind raced in circles. Had Monte heard, somehow, that she was searching for Annie? Had he bought her for Jo Lena, maybe to apologize, to try to make amends for leaving her without a word of goodbye?

All breath left her body. Monte had brought back her long-lost mare. *He* intended to get involved with *her*.

Monte gritted his teeth against the slight jarring of the mare's soft steps and gripped her mane to stay on. His body ached to fall forward and stretch out along her neck, but riding that way would hurt even more. He'd just have to hold on.

He tried to get his mind off his pain.

Soon as he rested up a little, he had to get back in shape. Why, Dexter, old and slow as he was, had had the mare out of the trailer before Monte could even get to the door.

And he'd be in the back room at Hugo's playing dominoes with the rest of the old men if he didn't watch it. However, right now, with the pain pounding him like a hammer on an anvil, that sounded pretty good. Maybe he should've stayed in the

15

hospital until the doctor let him out.

He was stiff as starched jeans and hurting like crazy. All he wanted was to crawl into a cool, dark place, ease his wreck of a body down and sleep for a week.

He jerked his mind away from that. Not yet. Not yet. He'd be horribly sore tomorrow if he slept out on the damp ground. If only he could avoid seeing anyone tonight.

Dexter never had been much of a talker. He'd been a neighbor to the Rocking M since before Monte was born, but he'd not be likely to call Bobbie Ann or Clint tonight to tell them about Monte being home.

Of course, sometime tomorrow they'd hear by the grapevine that he was back in the Hill Country. By then, he might be able to handle it, but not now.

Tonight all he wanted was to get into a bed of some kind, unheard and unseen.

A prodigal son needed to face one thing at a time when he returned, and for today this prodigal had already dealt with old friends and neighbors at the Bandera Cutting Horse Sale, the surprising sight of Jo Lena's old mare, Quick Way Annie, on the auction block, and the shock of the feelings roused in him by being even this close to home.

Tears stung his eyes. The arched sign

with the Rocking M brand in the middle had torn at him, but this familiar long, curving road with the pecan grove on his left and the bluffs rising to the right ripped away all his defenses. He was home.

For the first time in six years, with dusk falling around him, he was home.

Here he was, the great Monte McMahan, four-time champion of the Professional Bull Riding circuit, sneaking into his lair to recuperate from these injuries that had taken his life away.

Unsure of his welcome from his brothers, loaded with guilt at the sorrow he'd caused his mother and sisters, he was home.

Well, if he had to, he could camp out by the river and eat fish. Anything. Anything but more motels and more greasy spoon diners. *Those* he could not face anymore.

At the last curve before he could see the main house, he reined the mare off the road. They cut across behind the indoor arena and Manuel's house, headed for the river. Everything was quiet. Evening feeding was done, everybody had gone to supper.

The thought of food repelled Monte's stomach, which was sick from the pain. The mare didn't need to be fed, either, since she was used to being on pasture, the seller had said. He would put her in that five-acre lot behind the old bunkhouse and put himself inside it, assuming there were no hired hands staying there.

A door slammed somewhere and the faint sound of voices floated from the direction of the main barn on the still evening air, but no one saw him and he and Annie plodded on through the shadows of the trees to the river. Its murmuring soothed him a little as they moved upstream, passed behind the guest house and then saw that the old bunkhouse stood dark. At its back door, he dropped the bag to the ground, eased one leg over and carefully dismounted, his teeth clenched against the pain of the landing.

When Annie was safe in the fenced lot with grass and water, he walked stiffly to the bunkhouse, opened the back door and dragged his gear bag inside. He flipped a switch on the wall of the old, added-on bathroom and used the light to find a bunk. The place was bare. All the mattresses were rolled and tied.

He went to the closest one, took out his pocketknife, cut the twine and waited for the mattress to unwind and fall flat on the wooden bed frame. That was the last of his strength.

Miraculously, he managed not to fall. He sat down on the side of the bunk, eased himself back until he lay full length and fell asleep with his boots on.

Bobbie Ann finally gave up her fight for sleep and got out of bed at five the next morning. Something was happening or going to happen with Monte — she'd known that since early yesterday.

True, he'd been on her mind constantly since he got hurt again and every sportscaster on every PBR telecast had to speculate about whether or not he'd ever be able to ride again, but this was different. This was even different from that wild, clawing need that had tormented her — the need to go to Houston, to find his hospital room, to take him in her arms and beg him to come home and let his mother take care of him.

She hadn't done that because it would make Monte do just the opposite. If pushed, Monte would go to Brazil before he came home. So she had only called him and had kept her voice under control. Prayer and only prayer had given her the strength to do that.

Only prayer had sustained her since yesterday when the hospital operator had told her he was no longer there.

The phone rang as she was padding barefoot to the closet. She knew as she ran to get it that it was about Monte.

And it was. It was Jo Lena, the girl who used to love him, speaking in her husky voice, made even more husky by sleep. Jo Lena, the girl who could've made his life so different if he had *let* her love him.

"Bobbie Ann? Have you seen Monte yet?"

The phone froze to her ear.

"What are you talking about?"

"That's what I thought. He's on the ranch somewhere. When he didn't let Dexter drive him to the house, I figured he wanted to lay low for a while."

Quickly, Jo Lena told her what she'd seen and what she'd found out from a friend who'd seen Monte make the high bid for Annie at the Bandera sale. To which he had apparently hitchhiked from Houston.

"I would've told you last night, Bobbie Ann, but I was so . . . shook up, myself. And I knew he was too tired to face anybody."

Bobbie Ann brushed her hair back from her face with a hand that trembled.

"I did try to call him yesterday and the hospital people said he was gone."

Her voice was trembling, too, and she couldn't seem to stop it.

"Is it all right if I come over there this morning?" Jo Lena said.

"Of course! Anytime!"

"Please don't misunderstand," Jo Lena said. "It's the horse I'm interested in. I want her back. I wouldn't trust Monte as far as I could throw him."

The quick, sharp hope died, the hope Bobbie Ann hadn't even realized had been born until then.

"Sweetie, I understand," she said. "You have every right to feel that way."

They hung up, with no need to say any more.

Immediately, Bobbie Ann went through the house, the apartment in the barn and the guest house, seeing with the quickest glances that everything was undisturbed. She didn't see an extra horse anywhere. Only when she was headed back to the house, ready to call Manuel and tell him to go look for a campsite, did she think of the old bunkhouse.

She ran across the dew-laden grass, knowing in her heart what she would find. So, when she got there, she opened the door as quietly as the pink sun was rising on the new day.

Monte lay sprawled on his back on the bare, striped-ticking mattress, one arm out-flung above his head, the way he'd always slept as a child. His face was empty in sleep but the sunlight showed lines in his forehead, crow's feet beside his eyes and creases at his mouth. In fact, he was frowning a little bit — probably from a dream.

His open pocketknife lay where it had fallen from his dangling fingers to the floor.

Bobbie Ann sighed. Thirty-one years old and worn to a nub. Hard living and soul-racking pain had made her darling son old before his time.

But had they made him any wiser?

He was a feast for her eyes, though, no matter what.

He was home!

At least for this moment. Well, this moment was the only one she knew she had to live.

Thank You, Lord.

She leaned against the doorjamb, hugged her joy to her and watched him sleep.

Jo Lena Speirs leaned against the doorjamb, watching the baby sleep. No . . . Lily Rae. She had to quit calling her "the baby," had to quit even thinking of her as "the baby." Good heavens, the child would be five years old in the fall and she'd be going to kindergarten.

That old, familiar feeling clutched the pit of her stomach. Lily Rae was growing up, fast. Someday she, too, would leave her, the way Monte had done.

No, not the same way. Lily Rae would surely tell her goodbye.

The hurt stabbed her through to the bone, just as it had done on that day six years ago. She closed her eyes against it.

Dear Lord, please take this hurt away. Please help me know that what I feel for him now is sympathy and Christian love, not the kind of love I used to have for him. Give me Your strength and help me feel nothing at all when I see him today.

Jo Lena opened her eyes, shook her head and tried to banish the memories. What had happened to her vow not to give Monte any more power over her? Just because he was back in the Hill Country was no reason to backslide into thinking about him all the time.

If she'd married Monte, she would've only been settling just as she would have been if she'd married any of the other half-dozen men who had asked her over the years. She didn't need a husband. She had her faith in God, her child, her friends, her home, her work, her horses, and she didn't need anything else.

Except Quick Way Annie. She would get that taken care of today and then she would avoid Monte. The Rocking M was a huge place. She could ride Scooter and Lily Rae could ride Annie and sometimes Bobbie Ann would ride with them. Annie would be perfect for Lily Rae. Nothing like a seasoned, settled mount for a child to learn on.

It took all her self-control not to cross the room and wake the child up. She couldn't wait for Lily Rae to see her horse.

Monte had had a lot of nerve, anyhow, to even think of buying that mare. *Whatever* he intended to do with her.

Monte woke in a haze of hurting. His right arm lay above his head and a direct line of fiery pain ran from it down into his back. Every other part of his body either ached, agonized or tortured him.

The pills the doctor had given him in the hospital had worn off long ago and he had no prescription, since he'd snuck away on his own. He would have to tough it out except for the over-the-counter stuff he always carried in his gear bag for the usual aches and pains from bull riding.

For one long moment, he dreaded moving and creating greater pain, then, without stopping, he lowered his arm and began to try to sit up. He wouldn't think about it; he wouldn't let the pain into his mind.

It flowed in anyway, but he got to his feet in spite of it and staggered to his bag and to the bathroom. Ten minutes later, his face and hair wet by hasty ablutions performed while unable to bend over the sink, he stepped outside. He stood on the stoop and squinted in the sunlight.

Time to go up to the house. Time to face the music. Time to see his mom. He'd feel guilty at the sight of her, but she'd welcome him anyway.

Carefully, he stepped down onto the grass.

"Mommy, Mommy, look at me!"

The trilling cry of a child's voice stopped him. It was close, within a stone's throw. None of his siblings had a child, did they? A wave of disorientation swept through him.

Did they? How long had he been gone, anyhow?

He turned around and saw a golden-haired little girl, maybe four or five years old, standing on the bottom railing of the old wooden fence, leaning over, offering a handful of grass to Annie, who was ambling over to investigate it.

"She likes me already!"

Probably the child of one of the hired hands.

"I see you," a woman said. "Be sure to

hold your hand flat and don't let her get your fingers by mistake."

Jo Lena. It wasn't some woman, it was Jo Lena. The irresistibly husky voice was unmistakable.

Well. Chalk one up to the Hill Country grapevine. He'd expected word to get around, but not this fast — not Jo Lena Speirs on his doorstep first thing in the morning.

His breath stopped as she walked into his view.

Hair the color of honey, hair that felt like silk in his hands, hanging down her back in one thick braid. Hair pulled back from her beautiful face, tanned just a little from the sun. She was too fair to go without a hat, but today she wasn't wearing one.

She saw him then. Saw him and stopped dead in her tracks.

"Monte!"

Her voice vibrated with his name.

His heart racketed in his chest. Did she still care for him?

Cold reality killed that thought as the miserable guilt washed over him.

How in the world could she? He had left her without a word.

She remembered that at the same time he did. Her big, blue eyes narrowed and she

26

turned away from him to check on the little girl.

Mommy. The little girl had called her Mommy.

The strangest sense of loss came over him.

No, Jo Lena *didn't* still care. She hadn't cared for a long, long time. This child had to have been born within a year of when he left the Hill Country.

Now Jo Lena had her arm around the little girl and she was looking at him again.

"Monte, come and meet Lily Rae," she called. "We need to talk to you about Annie."

He walked toward them.

"Can you believe she just came through the sale?" he said.

"No, and I can't believe you bought her," she said, in a warm, cordial tone.

A tone that clearly said they were fine acquaintances and nothing more.

He walked up to them.

"Monte, I'd like you to meet Lily Rae," she said.

Lily Rae held out her hand like a grownup and gave him a straight look from her deep blue eyes. The very same shade of blue as Jo Lena's.

"Nice to meet you," she said in her piping little voice.

Well, her voice wasn't anything like her mother's. At least, not yet.

"Same here," Monte said.

Her smile was that of an imp. Her hand was tiny.

"Are you LydaAnn's brother?" Lily Rae seriously wanted to know.

"Yes," Monte said.

The little girl looked at him, considering.

"She already has two brothers."

Great. Even this kid who didn't know him thought he was unnecessary. He was home, all right.

"You don't think she can use another one?" he asked the child.

Lily Rae shook her head.

"Clint and Jackson are enough," she said decisively.

Then she flashed him a smile that looked so much like Jo Lena's — which he had not seen for years — it brought back a world of hurt.

"You can be *my* big brother," Lily Rae announced. "I don't have any and I need one."

He was so busy thinking about Jo Lena's smile from six years ago that it didn't quite soak in. And then it did. And it warmed a tiny cockle of his heart.

"Why do you need one?" he foolishly asked.

"To give me a hard time," she said. "LydaAnn says that's what brothers are good for."

A hole like a crater opened inside him. What had he missed in six years? He didn't even know his brothers and sisters anymore.

"It takes one to know one," he said, his voice suddenly rough with emotion. "LydaAnn can give a person a pretty hard time herself."

At least she used to. She must be a grown woman now. Had her personality changed, too?

"I know," Lily Rae said happily. "She's my big sister."

Then she turned back to the mare, stroking her nose and crooning wordlessly. Jo Lena had raised a happy little girl.

"How much are you asking for this mare, Monte?" Jo Lena said.

"She's not for sale."

Two pairs of blue eyes with identical expressions — worried, but mostly surprised — fixed on him.

"You can't be serious."

"Oh, but I am."

Jo Lena smiled. Lily Rae glanced at her, then went back to petting the mare.

"Everybody knows what you paid for her, Monte. Don't try a horse trade with me."

29

"I'm not," he said flatly. "I bought her to keep."

"Why? You're a bull rider, going down the road."

Used to be. I don't know what I am now.

"Bought 'er to look at," he said.

"Once every six years?"

"You sound downright sarcastic there, Jo Lena. It doesn't become you."

"As if I'm worried about your opinion," she said tartly.

Six years and motherhood seemed to have put a little edge on Jo Lena.

"You're trying to buy a horse from me that's not for sale," he pointed out.

"Look, Monte," she said earnestly, "I'll have to take out a loan to pay you what you paid for her. I'll do it and add a five-hundred dollar profit."

Her eyes were so blue. A deep, bluebonnet kind of blue. But she still hadn't smiled at him since the moment she saw him. Not a *real* smile, the way only Jo Lena could smile.

Suddenly, he wanted to see that smile. He *needed* to see it.

"Think about it," she urged. "You make five hundred overnight, and you aren't even out the gas money to haul her home."

"Remember when we helped Dexter vaccinate his goats for gas money?"

He got his reward. She smiled then, just like she used to.

For one, two, then three long beats of his heart, they looked at each other and Jo Lena smiled at him.

The smile made him feel like king of the world, just the way it always used to do. But she was different now. He didn't know her anymore. Deep down, she probably hated him.

If he had one grain of good sense left in his body, he'd let her have this mare and be rid of Jo Lena. Never see her again.

But the smile gave him a flash of power he hadn't felt for a while. Since before he got hurt and became a "victim" the first time.

He wanted, more than anything, to reach out and brush back the strand of straight, silky hair that had come loose from the braid. Like in the old days.

"So, Jo Lena," he drawled, teasing her, "exactly what is it you like about this horse?"

She lost her smile but she didn't break the look. The serious, no-nonsense expression came back into her eyes.

"I have some good memories and some bad ones," she said.

"Like what?"

31

"Oh, like when we had so much fun playing bareback tag in the pecan orchard in the twilight."

The memory hit him like a blow. It nearly stopped his heart.

"And the bad ones?" he said through the tightness in his chest.

"I hate it when somebody runs off from me," she said calmly. "Horse or man."

He wouldn't let himself look away. He made himself hold her gaze. He deserved that and more.

She was a woman now, Jo Lena was, with all her girlishness gone. A strong, beautiful woman he didn't know.

Give her the mare. He should give her the mare so she'd go.

"Jo Lena," he said. "This mare is not for sale. For any price."

"Bobbie Ann! Bobbie Ann!"

Lily Rae jumped off the fence and ran toward the house.

Monte and Jo Lena turned to see his mother on the back porch. And a vehicle coming down the road from the highway.

"Big family breakfast!" Bobbie Ann called. "Jo Lena, will you stay?"

Well. Forget the poor prodigal needing to face one thing at a time. First Jo Lena and now his brothers.

Lily Rae turned, yelling, "Please, Mommy, can we stay? Please?"

Jo Lena nodded yes.

Then she looked at Monte.

"Annie's my mare and you know it. Until we make a deal, I'm staying."

Monte looked at her straight.

"Well, I hope you brought your suitcase," he said. "I own her now and I'm not selling."

Chapter Two

The look she gave him then was enough to make him flash back through the last six years in a heartbeat. It was Jo Lena's famous, mule-stubborn, I-will-not-give-up-or-give-in look.

"I already have clothes here," she said. "In fact, I have my own room."

She turned her back on him and started for the house. He stared after her for a moment, then he caught up with her as fast as he could with his leg stiff and his back hurting like crazy.

His head was hurting worse, though. And he was losing his mind. Was this jealousy he felt, jealousy that she evidently was in his family and he was out?

No, it was irritation. Was he *never* going to be rid of her, even if he sold her the mare?

"You *live* here? Why? What about your husband?"

Jo Lena flicked him a glance and walked faster.

"I don't have a husband."

He *was* losing his mind. He knew that because suddenly, he knew what he was feeling — and it was fury. Some no-good rounder had left Jo Lena, who was a fine person in every respect, alone with a child to raise.

"Who is he, Jo Lena?"

She threw him another, more irritated, look and lengthened her stride. Jo Lena wasn't as tall as he was, but she had long legs and had always been able to match him, stride for stride.

"Who is who, Monte?"

"The bum who left you . . ."

Without slowing a bit, she turned and gave him another, sharper, more significant look. It stopped his tongue.

It nearly stopped his feet.

Well, yes, *he* himself had left her. But he hadn't married her and given her a child and *then* left her.

"Monte," Bobbie Ann called. "It is so good to see you, son."

He was close enough now to see the joy in his mom's face. His mother loved him. Even if Jo Lena had thrown him out of her heart before he got to the county line six years ago, and even if his brothers and sisters were still mad at him, his mother loved him.

"It's good to see you, too, Ma," he said.

35

Suddenly, it was true. So true he didn't know how he'd lived all those long days without seeing the love in her sparkling blue eyes. He went to her and hugged her, kissed her on the cheek. She held on to him for a minute.

The car drove into the yard behind him and the engine shut down.

"Here's your brother," she said. "Everybody's so glad you're home."

Warily, he turned to look. It really didn't matter which brother. Neither of them had any use for him.

Clint and Cait were getting out of a big, white SUV. He'd never met her, because he hadn't come home for John's funeral, but this must be Cait, who was his sister-in-law twice over.

Monte couldn't help but watch. Cait, clearly, was pregnant and Clint was positively tender as he helped her step from the running board to the ground.

He lost his tenderness, though, when he looked at Monte.

"Hey," he said. "Here's the prodigal son."

Cait gave Clint a quick look, almost like a warning, then she smiled at Monte.

"Are we ever glad to see you," she said. "I've been craving Bobbie Ann's biscuits and I hate to show up on her doorstep every single morning without an invitation."

They all laughed, Clint introduced Cait and she gave him her hand, then Clint shook with him, muttering, "It's about time you came home."

Monte thought about that as they all moved across the back porch and into the kitchen, milling around, trying to make small talk. It made him bristle. No doubt Clint and Jackson both would soon let him know, in no uncertain terms, where he stood with them, but he didn't care. He had a legitimate gripe about each of them, too, and if they didn't know what it was, he'd tell them.

Fortunately, Bobbie Ann took charge. She shooed Monte upstairs to his old room to shower and change, saying that breakfast would be ready in thirty minutes, and then she gave everybody else, including Lily Rae, a job to do.

Monte escaped gratefully. A shower would help clear his head and he would love the feel of clean clothes. Not to mention a chance to calm his heart about Jo Lena.

How could she have let go of him so soon? Let go enough to marry someone else and have that someone's baby within a year? It was still hard for him to believe.

Because that wasn't like Jo Lena. She had always been as loyal as she was stubborn.

Guilt stabbed him. He had hurt her enough to drive her straight into the arms of another man.

He must put the past out of his mind and deal with Jo Lena here in the present. Or not deal with her. He needed to get himself together and just ignore her. Avoid her.

His old room surrounded him peacefully. He sat down on the chair at the side of the bed, kicked the bootjack out from under it and stuck one heel into it, pulling carefully. Boots finally off, he began to peel the dirty clothes from his battered body, focusing on keeping his mind blank and all regrets and memories at bay.

This physical pain was enough to keep him busy. He had no need to dwell on his emotional hurts, too.

He levered himself up and went straight into the shower, standing for a long time in the tingling sluice of hot water, letting it relax some of his muscles and wash some of the ache out of his back. Soaping every inch he could reach without yelling in pain, shampooing his thick hair and rinsing took a long, blank time, and he was thankful for it.

Finally, he made himself shut off the water, step out and towel off. Cleaning up had made him feel a lot stronger.

And it actually made him smile to find that he still fit into his old, battered Wrangler jeans. He put on the most worn pair because they were the softest, and then, after clean socks and boots, his favorite, faded T-shirt he'd bought long ago when Billy Joe Shaver had played Gruene Hall and he and all three of his brothers had gone to hear him together.

Long ago and far away.

That opening line from one of the songs they'd heard started running through his head. Yes, that night seemed decades ago and thousands of miles away. But today it was now and he was here. On the Rocking M. Back home.

He had to go downstairs and face them — all but John, who was gone forever. John wouldn't be mad at him for not going to his funeral. John would take up for Monte if he were here this morning, even if they had been on opposite sides of the religion question.

He walked to the window and looked out over the ranch. John had been closer to him than to the others because for so long they'd been the young ones, bossed around by the big brothers. They'd staged their little rebellions, though.

Monte grinned to himself. Thinking

about John was driving away that shaky feeling inside him. He could hold his own with Clint and Jackson.

But then, while he walked carefully down the stairs and through the entry hall and the great room, he wasn't so sure of that. He just needed peace. And time alone. And an empty head.

And an empty heart. He didn't want to look at Jo Lena and see the girl he used to know and the woman he might never know all rolled up into one magnificent package that made his heart skip a beat.

She was the first thing that met his eye, though, when he crossed the threshold into the dining room. Jo Lena. And the rest of the women and babies. It didn't even seem like home, there were so many women and babies.

None of them belonged to him.

It was as unsettling as walking into a whole herd of unpredictable bulls to try to find his place at the table. There was a baby in a high chair on one side and Lily Rae on the other. His father and John were gone. Their absences screamed at him.

"Monte," Lily Rae called, the minute she saw him. "I want to sit by Monte."

Monte's jaw tightened. He ignored her.

Jackson looked up, saw him and they

limped toward each other to shake hands.

"Looks like you're about as bunged up as I am," Jackson said. "That must've been a whale of an argument you had with that bull."

"Ah, but you oughtta see the shape *he's* in," Monte said, and everyone laughed.

He felt himself relax a little as Jackson introduced him to his wife, Darcy, and Maegan, their curly-haired, red-headed baby girl with wide blue eyes the very color of Jackson's. Then Delia and LydaAnn were hugging him.

"Careful, girls, careful. Remember he's hurt," Bobbie Ann said, coming in from the kitchen with a big pan full of hot biscuits.

His sisters were careful with him. And they were telling him they were glad he was home.

But, as they let him go, they gave him looks that let him know they were pretty put-out with him for taking so long to *get* home. That was all right. They were truly glad to see him, even if they were probably going to give him a piece of their minds later on.

"Monte," Lily Rae said again. "I want to sit by Monte."

Bobbie Ann jumped right in, spoiling her rotten.

"Of course you can sit by Monte," she said, as she waited for Jo Lena to move one of the gravy bowls and a platter of sausage to make a place for the biscuits.

She looked up at Monte, her blue eyes sparkling with happiness.

"Son, will you sit at the end of the table? You've made a new young fan this morning."

"Monte's my big brother," Lily Rae, beaming, announced to the world in general.

"You better watch him," LydaAnn said, teasing her. "That Monte's full of tricks."

"Not as much as I am," Lily Rae said firmly.

Everybody laughed but she ignored that. She didn't care about getting attention right then because, small as she was, her whole purpose was to help hold the chair as Monte maneuvered his painful body into it.

Great. This was the final humiliation — being taken care of by a child.

"If that bull broke your leg, Monte, don't walk on it," Lily said, her piping voice cutting through all the rest of the conversation in the room. "I'll get you my grandpa's wheelchair."

"It's not broke," he snapped, much more harshly than he intended.

He clamped his mouth shut. This was ridiculous. Why wouldn't Jo Lena distract the child?

"But then, what would poor Grandpa do?" Jo Lena said softly.

"Use his walker," Lily Rae said earnestly, " 'cause he needs th' zexercise."

Bobbie Ann chuckled with the others, then she said, "My heart's so full this morning, I need to be the one to say the blessing."

Everyone bowed. Except Monte. He stared straight down the length of the table. He still was no hypocrite. And, six years later, it was still a fact that nobody was going to tell him what to believe.

"Monte! Bow your head," Lily Rae rasped in a loud whisper.

Startled, he shot her a fierce look. She glared right back at him.

Jo Lena gently laid her hand on the back of Lily's head and the child bowed it then, but before she closed her eyes, she gave Monte one last, sharp glance upward from beneath her long lashes.

In spite of his irritation, he had to suppress a grin. The kid had spunk — just like her mother.

Bobbie Ann said the blessing, thanking God for the food and for Monte's homecoming. Asking God to heal his body. Monte stared out the window behind his mother's chair and tried not to think about her words.

He would just as soon not be called to God's attention. Look at the shape he was in. His whole life as he'd known it was gone. God wasn't interested in him.

As soon as Bobbie Ann was done, Lily Rae piped up. "Monte didn't bow his head."

Everybody turned to look at him. He scowled at Lily Rae, which made everybody laugh but her.

Lily Rae, frowning worriedly, turned to Bobbie Ann.

"We have to teach him manners," Lily said.

That brought an even bigger laugh.

"Monte never did have any manners," Clint said. "We tried to teach 'em to him, didn't we, Jackson?"

"Sure did."

Bobbie Ann smiled at the little girl, then threw Monte one of her famous looks.

"Yes, we do, sugar," she said. "We'll work on his manners."

"Monte, why *didn't* you close your eyes during the prayer?" Lily Rae asked.

He busied himself crumbling biscuits and

drizzling gravy onto them. Maybe if he ignored her, she'd go away.

Maybe all of them would forget about him and talk about something else.

No such luck.

"Yeah, Monte," Clint drawled. "I'd think you'd want to bow your head and close your eyes and thank God for showing you the way home."

Monte's stomach tightened.

But not so much that he couldn't eat. This was the first home-cooked food he'd had for months. The gravy smelled heavenly.

"Ma," he said, "I haven't had a decent biscuit since I've been gone and no restaurant in the world can make sausage gravy like yours."

"Well, at least you remember Ma's cookin'," Jackson said. "For the last several years we were startin' to think you'd lost either your map or your memory."

Monte shot a defiant glance at him and then one at Clint.

He'd have to have it out with his brothers before too many days went by. But then, he had known that for six years now.

"Why do you have my mommy's horse?" Lily Rae said, attacking from another direction.

She *was* just like her mother. Same determination. She was going to make him talk to her, one way or the other.

He looked at her then, and tried his fiercest glare. Her wide, blue eyes never wavered. She took a big bite of a biscuit oozing with honey.

"Annie's my horse," he said finally. "I bought her at a sale."

Lily stared at him thoughtfully while she chewed.

He could feel Jo Lena's amused eyes on him. Delia's, too. Everybody was listening.

"Annie was my mommy's horse since she was a little foal," Lily Rae said as soon as she could talk again.

"Yeah," Delia put in, "she was. I remember when Annie was born, and when she was two I remember Jo Lena used to ride her."

Delia's voice was full of suppressed laughter.

Suddenly, aggravated as he was, Monte felt he was really home. Delia, at least, was going to treat him the same way she used to.

Well, to be truthful, so were Jackson and Clint, even if their baby brother was now thirty-one years old. Great irony in that.

He threw his sister a warning glance but, as always, she only laughed at him and

46

raised her eyebrows, demanding an answer as Lily Rae asked another question.

"Are you going to sell Annie to us?" Lily said.

If Jo Lena thought this mouthy little girl was cute enough to make him change his mind about that horse, she had another think coming. He hadn't bought the mare just so Jo Lena could own her again.

Matter of fact, at this moment, he couldn't quite remember the reason he *had* bought her. Maybe for old times' sake — memories had flooded through him like a river when he saw Annie come up the ramp onto the sale podium.

No. He had bought her for the foal she carried. The Quick Tiger and Sunny Meridian bloodlines could be a better cross to get a great cutter than most people might think.

"No," Monte said shortly. "There's no reason to sell her to you. You live on the same place with Annie and I'll let you ride her anytime you want to."

This shocked Lily Rae, who looked at him as if he'd lost his mind.

"Nuh-uh! Mommy and me don't live here. We live at our house!"

She turned to Jo Lena for confirmation.

Reluctantly, Monte stopped eating.

Thoroughly annoyed, he glared at Jo Lena.

"You said . . ."

"You jumped to conclusions," she said coolly. "I have my own room here — to change in. I ride nearly every day."

" 'Cause I like to play at Lupe's," Lily Rae said, naming the wife of Manuel, the ranch foreman. "She takes care of me and Maria."

She took a long drink of milk, holding the glass with both hands.

Then she smiled at Monte with her milk mustache shining above her lip.

"I can ride, too," she said, "and Mommy says Annie is a perfect horse for me."

His whole family was watching and listening as if this was a movie.

Well, too bad. Let them think whatever they wanted. They already judged him as selfish to the core, so he'd just prove them right.

"I'll let you ride Annie but I won't sell her," he said firmly. "Annie's a good mare and I have plans for her."

As those words left his mouth, he knew why it was that he'd bought the mare and why he was hanging on to her so fiercely.

It wasn't that he wanted to keep Jo Lena hanging around him from now on, begging to buy her.

Annie was nine years old and she'd never had a foal. She was possibly a great mare who'd never been taken to her full potential. She'd never even competed in a big cutting futurity. He could train her for that and he could see what he could do with her first foal.

She might prove to be the nucleus of a broodmare band he could build up — one that would be the best in the industry, bar none. He had a lot of winnings in the bank that he'd never had time to spend.

Yes, the reason he had bought the mare and the real reason he had come home was the same: he needed to prove himself where somebody who mattered could see it.

That realization was all Monte could think about after breakfast, when Bobbie Ann shooed her three sons out onto the back porch and firmly shut the kitchen door behind them. He did care what his brothers thought of him, much as he hated to admit he did.

And his sisters. And his mother. And Jo Lena.

He cared what all of them thought, even though he'd give anything if he didn't.

"Let's go over to the barn," Clint said. "Show Monte some winning horses."

"Good thing you didn't say winning *bulls*," Jackson said, but his tone was light enough that Monte knew he was teasing, not taunting, him.

"Yeah," Monte drawled. "I've seen enough winning bulls to last me for a while."

"When did the doctor say you could ride again?"

That was Clint. Always wanting to plan ahead, needing to get everything under control.

"That depends," Monte said evasively, "on a lot of things."

They walked toward the barn with him in the middle, carefully keeping to his slow pace, as if they aimed to keep *him* under control. Of course, Jackson couldn't walk much faster than him.

Which certainly wasn't fast enough to outrun the other subject on his mind.

"Say," Monte said casually, "who did Jo Lena marry, anyhow?"

They both looked at him.

"She didn't," Clint said, "far as I know."

Jackson shook his head.

"Jo Lena's never even dated much," he said. "Not since you left the county."

A whole new shock raced along Monte's nerves.

"No! That can't be."

"Why not?" Clint snapped. "Some women take things to heart. Maybe she can't trust any man after the way you did her."

Monte stopped in his tracks.

"Who is Lily Rae's daddy?" he demanded.

"Ray Don Kelley," Jackson said.

"Jo Lena's *brother-in-law?*"

"Yes," Clint said, exasperated now. "And her *sister's* child, you goober. Jo Lena's Lily's aunt."

"She calls her Mommy."

"Because Jo Lena's the only mother she's ever known," Clint said.

He gave Monte a narrow-eyed look.

"Are you still in love with her?"

Monte held the steady gray gaze with a hard one of his own.

"Not a chance," he said. "Just wonderin', that's all."

Jo Lena wished, for the hundredth time, that she'd never stayed for breakfast at the Rocking M.

"Can Monte come and see my room?" Lily Rae asked, as she crawled into her bed. "He can play with my Breyers horses if he wants."

If she could have ten minutes without

51

hearing Monte's name, she'd be happy. It didn't even have to be ten minutes of silence.

"That's sweet of you, Lily Rae," she said. "Now, let's read a story and you get to sleep. Tomorrow's Sunday school."

Lily Rae sat right straight up again.

"Is Monte coming to Sunday school?"

"I doubt it, sugar."

"Why not?"

Because Monte refuses to go to church at all.

"Well," she hedged, "Monte's in pretty bad shape, don't you remember? He can hardly walk, he hurts so much."

It hurt her, too, to think how much pain he was in. Even if she couldn't bear to hear his name one more time today.

"Monte could pray at Sunday school for God to make him all better."

"True," Jo Lena said. "But we can't decide for him what he should do. Monte has to decide for himself."

"We can help him, Mommy. We can teach him manners and bring him to Sunday school."

She had to decide what to do about Lily Rae's total infatuation with Monte McMahan, for heaven's sake. Like mother like daughter — it must be a female thing. What a mess!

"And *we'll* pray for him at Sunday school!"

Now the child was wringing her hands, she was so excited by this new thought. She had been in a total fit ever since they left the Rocking M and Monte behind.

"Lovey, stop talking now, lie back on your pillow and listen," she said. "I'm going to read to you now."

It took two stories for Lily Rae to relax and two more for sleep to come. Jo Lena was totally exhausted by the time she bent over to kiss the fragrant little face once more.

In spite of being so tired she could drop, she had made her routine last call of the day to the senior citizens' home to check on her father. Now, at last, she could relax. With a last glance in at Lily Rae, she eased the screen door open and went out onto her porch. She leaned against a post and looked up at the stars.

The way she and Monte used to do. Looking at the stars had reminded her of him every single night for six long years. If she hadn't had Lily Rae, she guessed she would've gone crazy.

No, she wouldn't have. Because God was the One who'd kept her sane.

And given her peace.

Now here was Monte come back, stirring up all the old feelings again.

Except that she wasn't going to let him do that. No matter how silly Lily Rae was about him.

Chapter Three

Sunday night Monte stretched out his aching body flat in the sweet-smelling grass and stared up at the stars. It was weird. It almost felt as if he hadn't seen the night sky since he left home all those years ago. When he used to look at it with Jo Lena.

He slammed his mind shut against the memories. He wasn't going to think about her, much less be around her anymore. He'd already enjoyed more of that than he could stand — especially with little Miss Mouth, Lily Rae, putting his personal life right out there on the breakfast table for everyone to see.

No, the reason being outside after dark was strange territory to him was the road. With all those weeks and years on the road, at night he was either riding in some indoor arena, falling exhausted into a motel bed, or driving or flying to the next place, readying his mind to get on the next bull.

Or else he was just so caught up in going

down the road that he never even thought to look up.

The river murmured along over its rocky bed a few yards away. Monte listened to it and let his gaze wander from star to star.

He himself had been a star. The commentators had talked about him on ESPN, the announcers had loved him and the crowds had chanted his name as soon as he'd climbed up the wall of the chute and started getting ready.

Monte! Monte! Monte!

Now he was nothing but a has-been.

A broken-up, broken-down has-been.

His only comfort was he wasn't broke. He'd been shrewd with his winnings, unlike ninety percent of the other guys on the circuit and he wouldn't have to ask his brothers for anything. Plus he had invested his inheritance from Grandpa Clint.

He grinned. Delia had always said Monte was wild in every way but with his money.

The Big Dipper blurred suddenly and he closed his eyes. Once again, he listened to the river run.

It was good to be on the Rocking M again, it was great to see his family again. But all of them, at different times, had been in and out of the big house, talking to him, asking him questions, expecting him to talk to them.

He had to have some space. He had to have some silence. He had to have a chance to get a grip on himself.

His life was gone. Life as he knew it, barring a miracle, could never come again.

Ever since he'd barely been a grown man he'd been a wild, wandering bull rider, living on the challenge, living on the danger, living on the satisfaction of staying on one of the crafty beasts until the whistle blew. The thrill of beating a bull somehow felt, every time, like one more little bit of revenge against the ugly, vicious one that had gored Scotty Speirs to death.

That had been a night with no stars, even though they'd been riding in an outdoor arena. That had been the night God turned his back on Monte. Monte had done the same to Him, and even Dad couldn't make him turn back again.

The thought of his father and his old friend stirred up grief and guilt that made his mind as bruised and sore as his body. It was too much to deal with tonight. He couldn't wait any longer for the oblivion of sleep.

Slowly, carefully, he rolled over onto his elbow and pushed with the other hand against the ground until he was in a sitting position. Laboriously, he inched on up to his feet and started toward the bunkhouse.

Good thing he'd told his mother he was going straight to bed. After the fit she'd thrown because he wasn't sleeping in the main house, she'd never get through scolding him for exposing his battered muscles to the dew-damp ground.

Which had been a major mistake.

Well, just as long as Bobbie Ann didn't see him right now, he was okay. Just as long as she and his sisters let him have a little peace, he might be able to figure out what he was going to do with the rest of his life.

They did let him sleep until he woke up on his own.

But they must've been peeping in at him every fifteen minutes because he had no more than pulled himself up and out of that last dream of being stomped by a bull and staggered out of bed to the bathroom than he heard the door to the bunkhouse bang open.

It was Delia and LydaAnn, judging by the giggling voices.

He did not feel one bit like giggling. Or listening to it, either.

"Throw me my jeans," he yelled through the closed door. "Looks like y'all could at least let a man get his pants on before invadin' his privacy."

"Looks like you could at least be pleasant to the women who brought your breakfast," LydaAnn yelled back.

He heard the slap of the rivets against the door as they hung his jeans on the knob. He opened it and reached around to get them.

"You didn't used to be so modest," Delia said. "I remember when you never would wear a shirt, even in the wintertime."

"When I was six years old!"

Carefully, very slowly, he began to lift one foot and try to fit it into one leg of his jeans. He caught a glimpse of his face in the mirror and nearly scared himself with his scowl. This was insane. If he didn't want to see his family, why had he come home?

Because he'd wanted a place to heal, not a party.

"Go on and wash up and try to pull yourself together," Delia called. "We took a thermos cup for 'em to put your coffee in, so it's still good and hot."

He heard rustling noises.

"I think your main surprise is still warm, too," LydaAnn said. "Can you smell what it is?"

He couldn't, but he realized then where they'd been. They were happy he was home and this was another welcome — they'd gone down the road to Hugo's to get the cinnamon rolls he had always loved. He ought to be ashamed of himself for being such a sorehead.

But the hard knot in his stomach only tightened and he took his time with his morning ablutions. He didn't have a choice about how long it took, did he? He couldn't move fast enough to catch a snail.

Finally, he raked his hands through his hair, tried to contort his face into some semblance of pleasantness and went out to meet them.

The sight did make him smile. There sat his sisters, each cross-legged on either end of his bed with a picnic of cinnamon rolls and coffee set out between them on a towel spread between the paper wrappings and the bare mattress. Bobbie Ann's daughters. No, if they truly were, they'd have brought a tablecloth and the good silver from the house. Then he noticed that they had real mugs for the coffee.

They'd dragged one of the old straight chairs out of the bunkhouse kitchen for him and set it on the floor halfway between them, facing the bed.

"So," he drawled, as he limped toward them, "I'm supposed to sit here in the hot seat?"

60

"Relax," Delia drawled back at him. "We won't jump on you too hard yet — we'll wait 'til you're able to defend yourself."

"Well, that's mighty good of you," he said. "I appreciate it."

"Everybody at Hugo's said to tell you 'hey,' " LydaAnn said. "Bill Ed Traywick wants to talk to you about when you rode The Twister."

Monte's scowl came back.

"What about it?"

"Bill Ed rode him, too, one time at the Mesquite Rodeo."

"Rode 'im or got on 'im?"

Both girls laughed.

"Got on him," Delia said. "Bill Ed said he never knew a man could spin so fast and not have his head torn off his body."

That made Monte laugh, too. A little. But he wasn't going to start hanging out at Hugo's, jawing with the boys. The very thought made him want to crawl in a hole.

Delia, who like Bobbie Ann was able to read a man's mind, watched him as he carefully sat down.

"Don't worry, Mont," she said, "we told them all that you aren't receiving visitors at this time."

"I don't know if Jennifer Taylor will exactly respect your wish for privacy, though,"

LydaAnn said, grinning widely. "She was remembering you fondly to everyone there. Something about a nighttime swim in the Guadalupe River."

"Jennifer Taylor was married before I ever left here," Monte growled.

"Well, she's not married anymore. And she told us twice to tell you 'hey.' "

Delia nodded.

"Jennifer would love even just one date so everybody could be talking about it," she said. "Her sister, Carrie, has gotten all the attention for so long."

"How's that?" Monte asked, just to be halfway polite.

But as long as his sisters were talking, he didn't have to.

"The money," LydaAnn said. "Did you hear about that embezzlement scandal at the courthouse? A year ago. Lots of people think it was Carrie who got the money, but if she did, she let Larry Riley go to prison for it."

"Yeah, Monte, surely you heard about that," Delia said. "The trial was on TV all over Texas. Remember — Carrie was married to Larry's cousin, Steve. That's how she got the job in the first place."

Monte got that swimming feeling in his head again. He reached for the coffee mug

LydaAnn was filling.

"Too much gossip," he said. "Y'all're makin' me dizzy. Give me a break, okay?"

They both frowned at him.

"Don't you even care?" LydaAnn said.

"No! And how come you even told everybody I was here?"

Delia shook her head and gazed at him with pity in her eyes.

"I could've kept you undercover if you'd called me to come and get you," she said. "But appearing out of nowhere at the Bandera sale and hitching a ride home for you and your horse *did* sorta put you in the public eye, brother dear."

He took a great gulp of the steaming strong coffee and immediately felt a little bit better.

"My mistake," he said, shaking his head. "What was I thinking?"

"We'd love to know," said LydaAnn.

The silence grew as she poured another cup of coffee and handed it to Delia.

"For the last six years we've wondered that very thing," LydaAnn said.

Monte's gut turned to concrete but he kept on drinking coffee.

"Hey, I thought y'all said I could get my strength back before I had to defend myself."

"We did," Delia said with a sharp glance at her sister. "And we will."

She folded back the foil that covered each huge cinnamon roll and passed them out with handfuls of napkins. Then, to his great amusement, she did hand around the good silver forks with the Rocking M brand on them. Monte relaxed a little and set his coffee on the towel so he could eat.

"A little bit of a social life will be good for you, though, Mont, whenever you're feeling a little better," LydaAnn said encouragingly.

He just let that slide. No way was he arguing with them about that now. These two were into music and barrel racing and cutting horses and fun of all kinds. They knew everything about everybody for miles around, and they'd be trying to drag him into all of their lives, too, just to make him feel at home.

"Thanks, I'll keep it in mind," he said.

What he had to do was feel *human* again.

In the middle of the morning, he was out in the pen behind the bunkhouse brushing Annie when his mother appeared at his elbow. He startled.

"If I'd been a snake . . ." she said, her smile bright.

It made him smile back at her, even though he didn't want any company — not even his mom.

"If you'd bit me, you'd have a bad taste in your mouth," he said. "I'm pretty sour."

"You're a sweet sight to me," she said. "I'm so glad you're home."

He liked to hear it but it made him feel guilty, too. And trapped.

"The place looks good," he said, and walked around the mare to work on her long, tangled mane.

As always, his mother sensed his mood.

"Well, I'll leave you to enjoy the sunshine and your new horse," she said, stroking Annie's neck. "I just came out to get your dirty clothes and put a load on to wash before I run into town. Can I bring you anything?"

It made him mad for her to start doing his laundry. Meddling in his business. Smothering him half to death. But he hated to hurt her feelings.

"No, thanks," he said, setting his jaw against telling her to let him take care of his own stuff. "I'm fine."

"When I get back, want me to help you move your things into the house?"

It sent a new jet of hot resentment through him. Why couldn't they all just leave him alone?

"No, Ma," he said shortly, "the bunk-house is great. I need some time to myself."

"Well, I don't want you to just sit out here and *brood*," she said. "Plus you shouldn't be alone right now. You're just starting to heal, Monte. You might get down and not be able to get up."

He gave a short bark of a laugh.

"Don't waste any of your worry on that. I've got so many visitors I can't get dressed in the mornings. I'm gonna have to start sleeping in my clothes."

She didn't say anything. Finally, even though he didn't want to, he met her searching, blue gaze.

"It's all *right*, Ma. Don't worry about me."

"We-ll," she said, "okay."

She turned to go.

"Sure I can't bring you anything?"

"Can't think of a thing I need," he said with a cheerfulness he didn't feel. "Thanks, anyway."

"All right," she said. "If you change your mind, call me on my cell."

With a final pat for Annie, she left.

Monte moved the currycomb in dust-raising circles along the mare's back. He might as well get ready for it — Bobbie Ann would never give up. She'd be after him again, later in the day, to move to his old room.

His resentment grew. Wasn't it enough that he'd come home? Did he have to live right in the family's pocket every minute, so they could make him feel guilty every second?

By noon Monte was in the main barn, hunting for his favorite old saddle while Annie stood tied to the hitching post right outside the door. It had to be somewhere in one of the narrow tack/feed rooms built off the main aisleway, but Daniel didn't know where and Monte wasn't going to ask anybody else. Daniel could be counted on to answer a direct question and go about his business. Clint or Jackson would have to hassle Monte awhile.

Saddles were stacked two and three deep on some of the racks, but he managed to lift them off each other and move them around until he found the one he'd always favored. He picked it up, snagged a pad to go under it, stepped awkwardly out into the aisle and headed toward the door.

He set his jaw against the pain. No way was he going to sit around and get so stiff and stove up that he couldn't do anything. No way was he going to let his body crater until he couldn't ride anything at all.

Bulls were one thing. He'd admit that. He might never be able to ride bulls again.

But horses were something else. And he had ridden Annie bareback in from the road yesterday, so he could certainly ride her in a saddle.

In a saddle, it might not hurt so much.

He made it to the door after having to stop and rest only once, and stepped out into the sunlight. Right into the path of Clint and Jackson.

"Well, hey, here's Monte," Clint said. "Up and at 'em at noon."

His tone was light, though, not derisive, and it held a note of . . . Was that pity?

Monte kept going, trying not to limp as much, hoping they wouldn't notice that the simple effort of carrying a saddle was making him break out in a cold sweat.

"Gonna ride your new mare?" Jackson asked.

He came straight to Monte and reached for the saddle. Clint glanced around, saw Annie and veered toward the hitch rack to get her.

That made Monte's gut tighten.

"I've got it," he said sharply. "I don't need any help."

His voice sounded weak, even to himself,

and slightly out of breath. Too much, too soon. He ought to sit down for a minute, but he'd been hurt worse and done more, and he could do it again.

Especially to avoid accepting help from his brothers.

Especially Jackson, who was more permanently injured than he was.

Jackson took the saddle anyway, even though Monte tried to hold on to it, and limped toward the mare with it. Clint led her to meet him and they met just as Monte reached them with the saddle pad.

"Look, guys, thanks," he managed to mutter, around the knot of fury and humiliation in his throat. "I can take it from here."

"Hold on," Clint said, saddling the mare with swift efficiency. "You tryin' to put us crossways with Ma? Daniel's over there by the indoor seeing every bit of this. We don't want him telling Bobbie Ann we let you saddle your own horse."

"Oh, sure, Daniel's a regular blabbermouth," Monte snapped. "Get away and let me on this mare."

Instead, Clint held her head and Jackson bent and cupped his hands to give Monte a leg up. He intended to ignore that and step into the stirrup instead, but when he tried, he couldn't raise his leg that high.

69

Suddenly, he remembered that yesterday he'd had to stand on Dexter's trailer and then wallow his way onto the horse. Seething, he accepted Jackson's help.

As soon as he was in the saddle, he took the reins, turned Annie's head and rode away.

Monte went in the back door of the guest house and walked around the game tables, between the rows of beds, past the open bathroom and kitchen doors into the spacious, comfortably furnished front room, which, along with the bathroom and kitchen, had originally been the entire guest house. The phone was still in its same corner, but now it was a cordless one.

He picked up the directory, found the name he wanted and punched in the numbers.

He was trying for his old buddy Chris West, but it was Chris's nephew, Dalton, who picked up on the second ring. He said Chris had gone to Ruidoso to visit his racehorses and wouldn't be back for a week and that he, Dalton, had just graduated from college and become Chris's partner. Naturally, they had to spend a couple of minutes getting acquainted. Dalton said he knew LydaAnn and had seen Monte on the PBR broadcasts and he kept calling him Mr. McMahan, but then, since a week was too long to wait, Monte got down to business.

"I want to buy a place, Dalton," he said. "Secluded as possible, some kind of a barn and a horse pen or two. What've you got listed right now?"

For a minute, all he got back was a stunned silence.

"You talkin' about *livin'* there, Mr. McMahan?"

"Right."

"Nothing . . . not a thing you'd want."

"Just a roof over my head. Running water. Electricity's optional. Whatcha got?"

"We-ell," Dalton said, "since you put it that way, there's the old Stoltz place. Do you remember it?"

"You bet. I used to coyote-hunt out there with your uncle Chris. Old Man Stoltz died?"

"Yeah. There's a renter in the little house but the big one's empty."

Then, Dalton got over his shock and went into true real estate sales mode.

"That house is a treasure, Mr. McMahan," he said. "Oughtta be on the National Register of Historic Places. Renovated, you could sell the place for a small fortune."

71

"Sounds good to me," Monte said. "Let's get it done."

That set young Dalton back again.

"Sight unseen?"

His tone was incredulous.

"I've seen it," Monte said. "Write 'er up. How about I go on and move over there first thing tomorrow and if we hit a snag of some kind, I'll just pay rent. How's that?"

Dalton might be a little slow sometimes, but once he got it, he got it.

"Perfect," he crowed. "Couldn't be better. Now, to negotiate the price . . ."

"What're you asking?"

Dalton gave him a number, Monte offered twenty thousand less and he jumped on it. That meant the old Stoltz ranch was in a whole lot worse shape than when Monte had last seen it, but he didn't care. He had to have a place where he could get his head straight. And that meant being alone.

Jo Lena flipped the switch to turn the big mixer on, glanced at the clock to time it and stepped up to the old butcher block where she rolled out her pie dough. She could get a couple of pie shells done while the mixer beat the cake batter.

As she worked the dough into a flat circle to get it ready for the rolling pin, she

72

glanced out the kitchen window. Ever since the phone message from Dalton West about the new buyer, she'd been watching the driveway as it wound up the hill. It had been nice not to have neighbors, but in a way it had been lonesome, too.

Yet, she didn't really want *neighbors,* except just to know that someone was nearby, someone to help in case of trouble. She didn't want anyone who might drop by in the evenings to take up her private time with Lily Rae.

In case she lost her to the Kelleys.

Her stomach clutched painfully. Ray Don's parents could not, simply could not, get custody of the child. She still had trouble believing that they would even try, when they never had before. But now Lily was old enough that they thought they could take care of her.

How heartless could they be, to try to wrench a six-year-old from the only mother she'd ever known?

She picked up the rolling pin and bore down with it, hard. If it came to a fight in court, she'd have to find a lawyer with a sweet tooth, someone who'd barter his services for a lifetime supply of pies and cookies.

Oh, Lord, give me faith. Don't let me even

think about it. Make them give up the idea, please, Lord.

She had to quit thinking about it. After all, worrying about the future was borrowing trouble and she had enough to cope with right now, in the present.

Lily Rae's crush on Monte. Somehow, she had to nip that in the bud. But she couldn't keep the child away from Lupe and Maria.

Dad's worsening mind. And whether the closest rest home was the best for him. Yet she couldn't drive very far to see him every day and still make a living.

Her business. It was growing so fast, she could barely keep up with the orders, but she loved the peace of working alone. And she really needed to save every penny in case she did have to go to court to keep Lily.

Trying to get her mind onto something else, she punched the CD player on with her elbow, then picked up the crust in her floury hands and laid it carefully in the deep-dish pie plate. Perfect.

Faith, Lord. Give me faith. Every one of these problems seems insurmountable, but You know the solutions. Send the answers to me, please.

Somebody knocked.

At first Jo Lena thought the sound was in

the backbeat of the music, but then she switched the mixer off. It came again. She must've missed the buyer driving in.

Hurrying toward the door, she wiped her floury hands on her apron. This would have to be quick. She certainly didn't have time to be giving tours of the ranch.

She opened the door.

"Monte?"

Her eyes were not deceiving her. It was Monte — all cleaned up and closely shaved, wearing starched jeans and a shirt and looking better than he ever had a right to.

One thud, and then her treacherous heart began to race. Stupid. She was as bad as Lily Rae. She had to grow up and remember how he'd treated her.

Just because the small green check in his crisp shirt with the button-down collar exactly matched his eyes, just because his short sleeves showed off the muscles in his strong, tanned arms, those were no reasons to forget that he'd left her flat without even a note and had never called her once. Not once in six years.

For a second, he only stared at her.

"How come *you* look surprised?" she said tartly.

He grinned and reached for the handle of the screen door.

"I don't know," he drawled, shaking his head in wonder. "After all, I'm old enough to know life's full of 'em. May I come in?"

"You'll have to if you want to talk to me," she snapped. "I've got muffins in the oven."

She turned on her heel and headed back to the kitchen. Then it occurred to her that he must've changed his mind about selling Annie to her. Therefore, she should try to at least be civil to him.

"I was expecting the new buyer for this place," she said, throwing the words over her shoulder. "Dalton West called and said if I saw somebody poking around the place that's who it'd be."

Monte's boot heels sounded on the hardwood floor right behind her as she went into the kitchen. They were still uneven, he was still limping, but he seemed to be getting around much better this morning.

"Why don't you pour yourself a cup of coffee and sit down over there at the table?" she said. "I'll be with you in a minute."

"Sounds good if you'll give me a muffin to go with it," he said, in an easy tone. "You know, I can't hardly drink coffee without something sweet to go with it."

Jo Lena reached for the oven mitt.

"What I know is that you are so pitiful," she said. "I'll give you a muffin."

She concentrated on taking the three pans of muffins from the oversize oven and dumping them onto the cooling racks set out on the worktable.

When she turned to carry the pans to the sink, he was staring around the room.

"Jo Lena," he said. "What are you doing here? Cooking for the whole county?"

Some irrational, totally insane disappointment hit her. He hadn't even been *curious* enough about her to ask Bobbie Ann what she did for a living.

"Just about," she said, turning on the water full force. "This is called a *business,* Monte."

Suddenly, she wanted him to know how successful she was. How well she'd done without him. How she was making a living for herself and her child by doing what she loved best.

"I supply the Hill Country Store and their ice-cream parlor with all their baked goods," she said. "And I fill private orders. I have more than I can do to satisfy the demand."

He opened the cabinet above the coffeepot, as surely as if he knew the cups would be there, and took down a large, blue mug. Thank goodness the ones they'd had made at the fair that time, the pair of matching mugs with their outlaw-costumed photos on them, were way at the back.

She did *not* want him to know that she'd hung on to a silly old souvenir of him all this time.

"Well, I can see why," he said, taking a deep breath of the wonderful aromas in the room. "This place smells like heaven."

"Thank you," she said primly. "Now, if you'll just take your seat at the table over there in the bay window, I'll get this cake in the oven and then we can talk."

He wandered to the worktable instead.

"Help yourself," she said as she poured batter into the four round cake pans she had ready. "Little plates are in that pie safe over there."

"No need for that," he said, his back to her, "I'm not used to fine china."

She focused on her task. Faded-out Wrangler jeans, starched to the hilt, should be outlawed.

Finally she slid the cake into the oven, he went over and sat down and she felt his eyes on her as she filled a mug of coffee for herself, snatched a muffin and a napkin, and went to join him.

"Now," she said. "Let's talk about Annie."

That flash of surprise showed in his eyes

again. Then it was gone.

"Annie," he said thoughtfully as he took another big bite of his muffin. "We've said all we have to say about Annie."

Her insanity kicked in again, just for a second, with the weirdest mix of feelings she'd ever felt. Had he come here to talk about them? About six years ago? And about now?

She took a sip of her coffee.

"Then what *do* we have to talk about, Monte?"

"You were right the first time," he said, holding her with a straight, steady look. "I'm the new buyer for this place, Jo Lena."

Chapter Four

Jo Lena went pale. She let her mug drop to the table.

She didn't even grab for it, and before Monte could set it upright and stop the spill, half the coffee was soaking into the crisp white tablecloth in a huge, fast-spreading stain. He couldn't believe it — Jo Lena didn't care. She didn't even look down.

Her eyes blazed at him, and if looks could start a fire, he'd have been toast.

"First my horse and now my house!" she cried.

The hurt in her voice slashed through his bones like a wild, cold rain.

"What'll you take next, Monte? My child?"

You already took my heart and broke it.

The words sprang to life between them although she didn't say them.

Her pain was so strong, it gave him a chill. It brought back all his old guilt and loss, and piled even more on top of it.

"What're you talking about? You think I bought this place just to torture you?"

Anger started flaming up through all the churning in his gut. "That's crazy!"

"Well, it'd fit the pattern, wouldn't it?" she said. "You've messed up your own life and now, all of a sudden, you're back here trying to crawl into mine or take it over!"

Her eyes blazed even hotter.

"*You* tell *me*. Exactly what is it you *are* doing, Monte?"

"Cut me some slack, Jo Lena," he said harshly. "I didn't even know you lived here."

Did she hate him so much? Did she think he was so low?

"Oh, sure," she said sarcastically. "Of course, you didn't."

"How could I?" he said, his voice hard as stone. "That kid nephew of Chris's doesn't know anything about us. He'd have no reason to tell me you were here."

"Your whole family knows where I live," she said flatly, as if she'd caught him in a lie for sure.

"My whole family doesn't know anything about this deal."

She narrowed her eyes and continued to stare at him as if he'd break down and tell the truth if she waited long enough.

"Look, Jo," he said harshly. "I didn't *care* who the renter was."

His anger expanded to include himself — because he cared this much about her opinion of him.

She finally let him loose from her scornful stare to glance around the room but not for long.

"No, I *don't* wish it!" she cried furiously. "I love this kitchen. And I'll tell you right now, Monte McMahan, that stove is mine, and so is the refrigerator. I had them both installed after I started getting so many orders, and I don't have time to move now even if I wanted to."

Her blue eyes hardened behind the tears. She slapped the table with the flat of her hand.

"You can just go buy another place. Get out of here and go find another ranch if you can't be satisfied with already owning half the county."

She pushed her chair back and stood.

"You heard me. Get out of my kitchen, Monte. And don't come back here."

She snatched up her cup and uneaten muffin and took them away then came back to pick up the small vase of wildflowers from the center of the round table.

"I've got to get this tablecloth in to

soak," she snapped. "Get up from there and go about your business and leave me to mine."

His legs would not move. If they did, he'd never be able to come back here again. He'd never see Jo Lena anymore because she'd never talk to him again.

He didn't even know why he cared if she ever talked to him again. He'd known it was all over with Jo Lena the minute he'd left the Hill Country.

No, in that horrible minute when Scotty never moved, even after the clowns lured the bull away from him. That was when he'd known it was all over with Jo Lena.

But now he only knew that if he walked out of this room he was lost.

As if he wasn't already.

"I'm not going anywhere and leave you thinking I'm conniving to ruin you," he said, masking his fear with an offhand tone and a careless gesture. "After all, I've got my reputation to worry about."

The surprised look she gave him helped his try at a smile. Then he swallowed, hard, around the knot in his throat.

For a second he thought she wanted to smile, too, but she kept her face blank.

"Your reputation," she said mockingly. "Oh, yeah, Monte. I forgot. You've always been really concerned about other people's opinions."

He picked up his mug and held it off the table.

"Go ahead," he said, faking confidence, "take care of that stain."

To his great relief, she pulled the cloth off the table and stalked away without another word.

He wracked his brain. She was right — he ought to get out of here and never come back. There was absolutely no point in staying because she'd never get over the fact that he'd caused her brother's death. Even if she did, he couldn't.

Monte got up slowly and walked to the counter, intending to set down his cup. However, he made the mistake of glancing up at his reflection in the mirror above the sink.

He turned his back on his image in a heartbeat, which sent a sharp pain shooting up his spine and into his shoulder. He blocked it out and gulped the rest of the hot coffee. Then he wrapped both hands around the empty mug and laced his fingers as if in prayer. What a joke.

If God existed, He had let Scotty die.

In the next room, water started hissing into the washer. The lid slammed down.

"Jo Lena," he blurted, as she came into the kitchen, "I never meant for *any* of it to happen. Not in the past and not now."

His heart was crashing like thunder in his chest. He never, ever, talked about any of it. Not to anyone.

She flicked him an icy blue glance and marched past him to the refrigerator. She opened the door, reached inside, brought out a carton of eggs, closed the door and turned around — all in one fast, efficient motion that was so totally typical of Jo Lena it made his stomach clutch.

"But you *do* mean to go ahead and buy this ranch, right?"

"I've bought it," he snapped, temper flaring again.

She strode to a long, battered table set against the wall and reached to the shelf underneath it for a bowl. Then another bowl.

"So I can either deal with it or move. Is that the choice you're giving me?"

She began cracking eggs and separating the yolks and whites. Quickly.

"A person sets up his own choices," he said.

Her hands slowed, then stopped, as she turned to look straight at him.

"That's right," she said. "And you made yours."

He held her gaze with his.

The hurt in her eyes, and especially in the set of her shoulders, tore at his conscience, yes. But her pain was worse than his guilt right now.

He swallowed hard. If it'd ease her any, he'd make himself talk about it. If he could find how to begin.

Finally he spoke.

"I didn't choose for Scotty to get killed," he said.

She looked at him for a long moment.

"No," she said slowly, "you didn't. But you chose to leave me at a very bad time in my life."

The shock of hearing that stopped his breath.

He couldn't think.

He couldn't know what it meant.

Had she forgotten that he had been the *cause* of that very bad time in her life? Back then, she couldn't stand the sight of him. She'd be seeing him on the Rocking M and around town. And, occasionally, no doubt, here on this ranch. She could get used to it — for her own good.

"Well, I'm back now, Jo Lena."

In a rush of wild thoughts he pondered how he might be able to make things up to her, make one small compensation for all his sins. He could keep this ranch and be her neighbor. It had been on the open market. What if some drug dealer or child molester had bought it?

"Yes," she said coldly, "you're back now. I can't argue with that."

She turned to her work.

"I'm here and I'm staying," Monte said, a new calmness coming to him. "These houses are two miles from the road and five or six from the nearest neighbor. Anybody could've bought this place. You're better off with me."

She set her jaw and flashed him a look as she broke another egg.

"In your opinion," she said dryly.

"Any sane person would agree," he said, his heartbeat slowing and his breath growing steady with his purpose. "A woman and a child living out here alone need some protection."

She finished separating the egg and dropped the shell onto the pile she'd started on the table.

"Give me a break, Monte," she said, and went to get the trash sack out from under the sink. "You're only torturing me for my own good. Is that what you're saying? You're buying an expensive piece of real estate so you can become my protector and

87

keep the bad guys away? I thought you didn't know I was here."

Her arm brushed his leg as she opened the cabinet door. She jerked away as if he'd burned her.

Her scent filled his nostrils, that light drift of flowery fragrance that struck such a chord in him it tightened all the muscles in his throat. He wanted to reach out and pull her to him, just stand there with her in his arms and breathe in the smell of her hair.

But he couldn't. Never again would he have that comfort.

"I *didn't* know you were here," he said, his anger trying to flare again.

He held it down, though, and concentrated on *her* feelings, instead. He wanted to reassure her, wanted to lessen her pain if he could.

"I'll live in the big house," he said. "That's a hundred yards away. Y'all don't ever have to see me."

"As long as Lily Rae doesn't know you're there," she said indignantly. "Why do you have to complicate my life like this right now when I've already got more than I can say grace over?"

With three long steps she was back at the worktable. She swept the eggshells off into the sack.

"Look, Monte," she said in a tone so carelessly final, it made his skin crawl, "with God's help, I can take care of myself and Lily Rae. I've been doing it for years. Don't try to fool me or yourself by making up an heroic excuse for this latest interference in my life."

When she straightened up and squared her shoulders, her blue gaze held steady on his.

"I don't understand what you're doing or why," she said. "And I can't stop you, Monte. No way would I ever have the money to buy this place. But the fact that I'm not leaving this house doesn't mean that I'm letting you into our lives. Is that clear?"

"All right," he said, frustration churning in his stomach as he turned carefully to set the mug in the sink. "I don't blame you for holding the past against me."

"I have work to do," she said, standing perfectly still, waiting for him to go.

So. She wasn't going to talk about it. Fine. He didn't want to talk about it, either.

His anger flared again, but he gave her a long, straight look just like the one she was giving him.

"I'll be right next door, Jo Lena," he said calmly. "If you need anything, feel free to call."

He strode to the chalkboard on the wall next to the back door, picked up the piece of chalk dangling on a string.

"Here's my cell phone number," he said, writing it in big numbers beneath the grocery list.

She didn't say a word.

When he finished, he let the chalk swing free again and turned around. He walked past Jo Lena and through the doorway, out of the sweet-smelling kitchen into the square, high-ceilinged living room. If she believed he was trying to interfere in her life, if she stayed strictly away from him, well then, that was no more than he deserved.

However, now she should know different. All she had to do was look at her blackboard and see that she'd have to call him — he wasn't going to call her.

At least she had given him a whole new reason to get up every day: to prove to her that he had no interest whatsoever in any part of her business or personal affairs. After all, hadn't he bought this ranch in the first place so he could have his privacy?

Giving her hers would be no problem at all.

To Jo Lena's great relief, Monte's truck was nowhere in sight that evening when she and Lily Rae drove the winding road up the hill to their house. He had been in one of the white Rocking M pickups — the smaller extended cab, not one of the four-doors. She'd seen that much when she carried her finished baked goods to her battered blue Explorer and set out on her afternoon's deliveries.

At that time the vehicle had been sitting in front of his house. Now it must be back by the barn.

Actually, it didn't matter where it was as long as Lily Rae didn't see it tonight. It had been a long, long day.

Jo Lena held her breath as she covered the rest of the distance to her house and started turning into the spot nearest the kitchen door where she always parked. It was nearly dark, much later than usual for the two of them to be getting home. There weren't any lights on in Monte's house that she could see from here.

Her heart started a rapid drumbeat. Maybe he'd changed his mind. Maybe the house had been in such bad shape he'd decided not to live in it. Maybe Bobbie Ann had begged him to stay on at the Rocking M and he'd given in.

Maybe, just maybe, instead of waiting until tomorrow to tell Lily Rae that her precious Monte would be living next door — maybe she'd never have to tell her that at all.

Her hopes began to rise as she put the car in park and shut off the motor. Maybe the Lord knew that she didn't have enough strength to deal with Monte as her neighbor.

All the while she and Lily Rae ate their supper and she got the child into her bath, she encouraged herself to believe that Monte had changed his plans. He just had to. His visit this morning had put her into such a fit of imagining the future and re-membering the past that she had put too much vanilla in the cake frosting and nearly browned the pies' meringues beyond ac-ceptability.

If she had to try to keep Lily Rae away from him — with him right next door all the time — she was liable to lose her mind com-pletely.

She did *not* still love Monte. She had only thought she did. What she had felt when she saw him get out of Dexter's truck and crawl up onto Annie's back was compassion. Anyone with half a heart would've felt the same.

Her pulse raced like mad, though, when she remembered how he'd looked this morning, all cleaned up and clear-eyed.

Angry as she'd been at his invading her turf, she'd wanted to reach out and touch him the whole time.

Jo Lena pushed that thought away as she finished turning down Lily's bed, found her favorite book and started toward the door to go get her out of the bath. Lily was singing, splashing mightily in the tub full of water topped with bubble bath, pretending that she was taking her Breyers horses over jumps instead of over mountains of pink foam.

She shook her head. Lily was going to protest, but she had to get out of the water now and get to bed. Tomorrow would be especially busy — twelve dozen cookies for an afternoon tea at the library. Jo Lena wanted them to be ultrafresh and delicious because all the prominent hostesses for miles around would be there.

As she stepped through the doorway into the hall, she was trying to think how early in the morning she should take Lily Rae to Lupe's.

The lights went out.

Just like that, all over the house. Instantly, the inside of the house was as black as the outside where there was no moon.

"Mo-om-my!"

Lily Rae's cry ended in a screech.

93

"I'm coming, honey."

Jo Lena put her hands out in front of her and started feeling her way.

"Just stay right where you are, baby. Stay there, 'cause there's water all over the floor and you might slip."

"I dropped Skeeter!" Lily wailed. "Now he's about to drown. I have to find him."

"No, wait 'til I can help you," Jo Lena cried, visualizing Lily Rae with her head underwater searching for the plastic horse.

"Wait, baby, and we'll find him together."

"I'm not a baby! I'm big!"

"Of course. I know you are but even big girls need help sometimes. I'll be there in just a minute."

Her bare toe struck something and she remembered, too late, that she'd moved the clothes hamper out of the tiny bathroom the day before. She bit her lip against the exclamation of pain so Lily wouldn't hear it and try to come to her.

"We'll get Skeeter as soon as we turn on the flashlight," she called.

Her blood thundered in her head. Where was the flashlight? She usually kept one beside her bed but she didn't recall seeing it there lately.

She couldn't go look for it, either, until

she had Lily out of that deep water and in her arms.

"Lily?" she called, trying to keep her voice level. "What are you doing, honey?"

No answer.

Jo Lena hurried even more and finally slammed one extended arm against the jamb of the open doorway. She hurtled through it.

"Lily! What are you . . ."

"I got him! Mommy, Skeeter's not drowned."

"Well, thank goodness," Jo Lena said with all the sincerity of a prayer, which it was. "Let's find your towel, sweetheart, and get you out of that water. We'll have to rinse you off later."

"He's snorting the water out of his nose," Lily said. "I think he *nearly* drowned."

A strange gleam of light glowed on the horizon and Jo Lena looked out the small, high window. Her heart sank as she saw it came from farther up the hill, from the lights in Monte's house, which she'd never seen turned on before.

The sight made her want to cry. He had moved in, after all.

Her whole body wanted to collapse in despair. But she couldn't let it. She couldn't even think about the future. She had to get this child out of the tub and get the power back on.

She had to think about the problem at hand. This wasn't a general outage. It was her house and she had to do something about it.

She slowed down when she reached the section of floor near the tub that had water on it. She felt for the towel she'd hung on the rack and found it.

Well, one thing she knew for certain, she wasn't calling Monte's cell phone number for help. The rural electric company would send somebody.

Dear Lord, please let them get the power back on tonight. I have to have the mixer working or I'll never get all the cookies done.

"Where are you, sugar?" she said, forcing herself to deal with one thing at a time. "Here's your towel. Let's wrap you up in it and go call the electric company."

Lily Rae came into her arms. Jo Lena wrapped her cozily in the big towel and hugged her close, loving the small, wet arms clasping her neck. She pressed her cheek against the child's sweet-smelling hair, half-dry now, since she'd stayed in her bath for so long.

For another moment Jo Lena held her, staring over her head and out the window.

It hit her then. There were lights burning in Monte's house for the first time. There were none in her house — for the first time.

She wanted to scream.

No. She would not call him, she would not involve him. She'd take care of herself and she would not *ever* use that number he gave her. She'd meant to erase it but she just hadn't gotten around to it.

Jo Lena turned away from the window, squeezed Lily Rae even more tightly and felt her way toward her bedroom.

"Mommy, you're mashing Skeeter and Susie."

"Sorry, honey."

She loosened her grip and kept going, out into the hall, then to the right.

Her eyes were getting adjusted and she could see a little bit. All she had to do was find the flashlight, the electric co-op's number and her phone. They'd send somebody out really fast.

She reached her bedroom, sat down on the side of the bed with Lily in her lap and started feeling around for the flashlight.

"Now where could I have put it?" she muttered.

A loud pounding on the front porch answered her.

"Jo Lena! It's me! I saw your lights go out!"

"Monte!" Lily Rae screamed. "Mommy, it's Monte!"

She scrambled free of Jo Lena's arms and ran around the foot of the bed, heading for the door that opened directly into the living room.

"Careful!" Jo Lena called. "Don't run into something. I'm coming, Lily. . . ."

Too late. The door swung back and a lantern, closely followed by Monte, came into the house.

"Need some light to get to the door?" he said.

"Monte!" Lily Rae cried. "Did you come to fix our lights? Can you turn them back on?"

"I'm here to try," Monte said in that rich, low voice that used to make Jo Lena go weak all over.

She closed her eyes in despair. Why, *why* couldn't he have just stayed away? Why, when he could've bought any property for sale in the state of Texas, had he bought this one?

Jo Lena threw herself to the floor on her knees and felt farther under the bed for her flashlight.

"I'll help you! Can I help you, Monte?"

Now Lily Rae would be so hyper she wouldn't go to sleep for hours.

"I suppose. But first, let's get your mommy to help us both."

"Mo-om-my!"

Jo Lena touched the flashlight. She closed her hand around it, pulled it out, stood up, snapped it on, then walked toward the living room brandishing it as if it were a weapon.

"You shouldn't have bothered," she said coolly. "I have a flashlight and I'm calling the co-op right now."

"No bother," he said.

The lantern's glow threw his face into shadow but it limned his cheekbones and made his eyes flash in the dark room. It made him seem very mysterious.

Very handsome, too.

He wore a white T-shirt and the muscles in his arms strained against the tight sleeves.

"Monte," she said sharply, "I told you I can take care of us."

He ignored that.

"Do you have a fuse box?"

"Yes."

He gave a disgusted snort at her uncooperative answer.

"Where is it?"

"Out on the back porch."

He started in that direction, Lily Rae leaped to follow and Jo Lena, of course, had to go with them.

"This box must be for the barn and your house," he said. "As soon as I switched on the barn lights I saw yours go out."

"I don't like you watching us," she said sharply. "I thought you said you wouldn't."

Lily Rae was now wearing her towel like a sarong, walking proudly along between them. She gave Jo Lena a mild glance up and over her shoulder.

"Is that your kind voice, Mommy?"

For once, Jo Lena ignored her child. She was just so furious and so exhausted that she would burst into tears if it'd do any good.

Monte chuckled.

"Yeah, Jo Lena, is that your kind voice?"

"Compared to the one I'd *like* to use? Yes."

Monte laughed. He actually laughed and Lily giggled.

Jo Lena sighed. She'd known the minute she saw him get out of Dexter's truck there'd be nothing but trouble.

Chapter Five

They followed on his heels right through the dark kitchen, with Jo Lena shining her flashlight ahead of him as if his lantern wasn't already showing the way. Typical. She wouldn't let him help her if she could possibly jump in and do it herself.

There was only one problem with that: she didn't know what to do or she would've already done it.

Of course, to tell the truth, he didn't know, either — not for sure — but he didn't have to tell her so.

"Save your batteries," he said. "We may need 'em. I don't know how old mine are."

She shut her light off.

"Well, I hope we don't have to depend on batteries for very long," she said indignantly.

"Not past sun-up," he said.

"Very funny, Monte."

"And true, too," he said.

He didn't quite know why he suddenly felt more lighthearted, but he did.

However, Jo Lena didn't share that. She was tense enough to walk the fence.

"My power has to be back on by morning if it takes you all night," she said. "I have to make twelve dozen cookies and deliver them to the library by two tomorrow afternoon."

"No problem," he said. "We aim to please."

"We aim to please," Lily Rae echoed happily.

"We also have to get you into bed, missy," Jo Lena said. "Just as soon as we find out what the problem is."

"N-o-o," Lily Rae wailed. "I want to see Monte fix it!"

"Probably we just blew a fuse," he said. "Won't take a minute to replace it."

"Well, if it does take longer than that, you have to go to bed, sweetie," Jo Lena said quickly. "You were already exhausted when you got into your bath and I let you stay in there way too long and now it's nearly eleven o'clock."

"But I can't sleep in the *dark!*"

Jo Lena chuckled but she didn't sound very sincere.

"Lily Rae Kelley," she said firmly. "You sleep in the dark every night."

"I want my My Little Pony night-light," Lily said, whining a bit. "I can't sleep without my My Little Pony night-light."

"Yes, you can," Jo Lena said firmly.

"No, Mommy. I can't."

Monte didn't know much about kids, but this sounded like the beginning of trouble. And Jo Lena sounded pretty ragged around the edges.

"Mmm-mmm, what smells so good in here?" he said as he led the little procession to the back door. "Is it cinnamon?"

"Yes," Lily Rae said, obviously thrilled to change the subject from bedtime to anything else at all, "it's cinnanmum. Do you like cinnanmum, Monte?"

"Sure do," he said. "Your mommy knows I love cinnamon."

"Yes, Monte, I know you love cinnamon . . . and doing *whatever* you want *whenever* you want . . ." Jo Lena said, barely keeping the sarcasm to an acceptable level.

"I love cinnanmum, too, Monte," Lily Rae said happily. "You're my big brother and we both love it."

". . . no matter how much trouble it might make for somebody else," Jo Lena finished.

Those words sliced him to the quick. She couldn't possibly know how true they were.

Distraction. That was the ticket. For him as well as for Lily Rae.

"Now, now, Jo Lena," he drawled, "how

103

come you're so put out with me? All I'm doing is trying to help."

"I didn't *need* any help until you moved into the neighborhood," she said in such a tart tone, he couldn't help but grin.

It had never been difficult to get under Jo Lena's beautiful skin. At least not when it came to aggravation.

Lily Rae let out a squeal that made the hair stand up on the back of his neck.

"You *moved* here, Monte? You moved here from the Rocking M?"

"Yep," he said as he opened the back door and they all trailed through.

Lily started whirling around in circles, bumping into him, then into Jo Lena in the small space of the back porch.

"Yay, yay, yay," she chanted. "Yay for Monte. Yay for Monte. Monte lives with us. *I* get to tell LydaAnn."

"Not *with* us," Jo Lena said sharply. "Next door to us."

"In the big house?"

"Right," Monte said.

"Yay, yay, yay! Monte lives in the big house."

Jo Lena gave a huge sigh. "Now she'll be too excited to sleep," she said wearily. "I don't know when I'll learn to keep my mouth shut."

"Not your fault," he soothed, setting his lantern on top of the washing machine. "She was already excited just because I'm here."

"Well! You are as conceited as ever!" Jo Lena snapped.

"Just the truth," he drawled, turning to grin at her over his shoulder as he reached for the door of the fuse box. "Too bad I don't excite the grown women like I do the little girls."

"Oh, I'm excited, all right," she drawled back. "I haven't had this much excitement in one day since I can't remember when."

Her sarcasm didn't matter. Neither did the fact she was wanting to get rid of him. Somehow it just felt good to be this close to her, to feel her standing right behind him, waiting to see what he would do to get her out of this jam. Her breath felt warm where it brushed past his neck.

He opened up the box and shone his light on the rows of fuses inside.

"These are the real old-fashioned kind," he said. "Where do you keep the extras?"

"I don't have any," Jo Lena said. "I've never even looked at them before."

"Hmm," Monte said mildly as he checked the connections. "Wish you had some."

"So do I," she shot back defensively. "If

105

I'd only known, I would've stocked up."

"I think that one there is blown," he said. "But I'll never be able to get a new one tonight."

"At Wal-Mart we could," Lily said, jumping up and down. "I know! Let's all go to Wal-Mart!"

"They won't have this kind," he told her. "I'll have to go to a hardware store in the morning."

"I cannot believe this," Jo Lena muttered desperately. "I *have* to have power in this house, and I mean *early*."

Her quiet panic made Monte feel bad, but it made him feel good, too. This was the first problem he'd caused Jo Lena that he could actually fix.

"Monte . . ." she began.

"Don't worry," he said. "I'm sorry I messed you up. But I'll have all your equipment up and running right after daylight, I promise. I'll call Old Man Donathan and ask him to open early."

"The oven's gas," she said. "It's the mixer I need."

"You'll have it," he promised.

Lily was still dancing in circles, singing to her plastic horses as she twirled them in the air. "Monte's my big brother. Monte's my big brother."

She was getting louder by the minute.

"You've got to get into bed," Jo Lena said over the noise.

Lily pretended not to hear and sang even louder.

Jo Lena took her by the shoulders and started herding her toward the kitchen door. She turned to Monte.

"We've got our flashlight," she said. "We'll be fine. Thanks for trying. Good night."

"No-o-o," Lily cried. "It's *dark!* I want my My Little Pony. . . ."

"I know, I know," Jo Lena said, "but you'll have to do without it tonight."

"I want Monte," Lily wailed. "Don't send him home."

She burst into tears just as he stepped into the kitchen behind them.

He held up the lantern and looked over the situation. Jo Lena looked ready to cry, too.

"Let's go get you into your nightgown," she said, scooping the little girl up into her arms. "That'll make you feel better."

"Monte," she said, turning to him, "you can find your way out, right?"

"Listen," he said. "I'm not leaving y'all here alone. Come up to my house. Bring your night-light and . . ."

"Yay!" Lily cried. "I'll go get it."

Immediately she scrambled down and ran into the dark living room. Jo Lena turned on her flashlight and shone it in that direction.

"See?" she said hotly. "She's not afraid of the dark! *Why* did you have to get her all wound up again, Monte?"

"Because I mean it," he said flatly. "I'm not leaving you two alone down here. You might have an emergency."

She didn't answer for a minute. He could practically see the wheels turning in her head. At least she remembered him well enough to recognize when he was being as stubborn as she was.

"If we went to your house, where would we sleep, Monte?"

She sounded honestly amused.

He felt a small success. At least he'd taken her mind off her troubles.

"Do you even have linens on the beds?" she said.

"We-ell, actually, now that you mention it . . ."

"You have no beds, right?"

They both laughed.

"Right. But I could let y'all have my sleeping bag and —"

"The floors in that house need to be shoveled out and mopped with soap and water,"

Jo Lena said. "I'm not putting my clean quilts down in that dirt."

Monte looked into her eyes. The lantern light played on her beautiful face. Tired, drawn, mad, stubborn — it didn't matter. No woman on earth was as beautiful as Jo Lena.

"Then I'm staying here," he said.

"That's ridiculous! We're alone every night — sleeping in the dark. We have a flashlight. We'll be fine."

She looked back at him for a long moment, silent.

Too tired to argue, probably, although she'd never admit it. Or else she thought she'd won the battle and he'd go away.

He wanted to kiss her. Instead, he lifted his free hand and brushed back a strand of her hair that had come loose from her braid.

"Here she is," Lily Rae called. "Monte, now you can see my My Little Pony night-light."

Lily, now wearing a nightgown instead of a towel, came flying back toward them through the cone of light Jo Lena held for her.

"She's too little to ride," she said. "She's my guard pony."

Monte squatted on his haunches to be at eye level with her and set the lantern on the floor. She held out a pink plastic pony with a flowing tail and a plug-in on the back. Under her other arm, Lily Rae carried a wadded blanket.

"I think she's a quarter horse," Lily said.

Monte considered.

"Looks like one to me," he said. "What color would you call her?"

"A pink roan," Lily said decisively.

She took back the pony.

"Okay," she said. "I'm ready to go to your house. Will you carry me, Monte? I'm barefooted."

She came closer, holding up her arms as best she could, considering her burdens.

Monte picked her up and held her in one arm while he grabbed the lantern with the other.

Jo Lena heaved a great sigh. She stroked Lily's blond hair, tucked it back behind her ears.

"Monte's floors are too dirty to sleep on tonight, sugar," she said.

Lily leaned her head against Monte's cheek as if to tell him not to worry about his floors, and looked at her mother.

"Are his beds dirty, too?"

Monte suppressed a grin.

"He doesn't have any beds," Jo Lena said.

Lily Rae looked at him.

"You mustn't sleep on the dirty floor," she told him. "You can sleep at our house."

He winked at her.

"That's exactly what I told your mommy."

Jo Lena groaned.

"I'm *not* scared, Monte," she said. "Go on home and get some rest. You have to rest for your back to heal."

"*I'm* scared," Lily Rae said, winding her arms around his neck.

Jo Lena closed her eyes and appeared to be praying for patience.

"And Monte can't sleep on his dirty floor, either," Lily Rae announced in a tone so much like Jo Lena's, he had to smile. "It's not good for him!"

She leaned back and smiled at him.

"You can have my bed, Monte," she said. "It's not very big, but you can have it for your back."

"I tell you what," Monte said quickly. "How about we have a camp-out in the living room? Are y'all's floors clean enough to put down some quilts?"

"Yes! Mommy cleaned them!"

Lily Rae started bouncing on his arm, poking his neck with the night-light at every jump. "Let's put our sleeping bags on the *clean* floor!" she crowed. "Let's all sleep on the *clean* floor!"

She started slithering out of his grasp.

"I'll get the pallet!" she said, and ran out of the kitchen again. "Come on, Monte, bring the lantern!"

Jo Lena hadn't moved.

"Sneaky snake," she said.

She didn't sound really mad, though.

"Aw, come on, Jo," he said. "You know you were going to say yes anyhow."

"No matter what I said, you know you were going to stay."

They knew each other pretty well. Still. After all these years.

Jo Lena kept thinking that as she supervised the pallet making and finally got to stretch out under the sheet Lily Rae had chosen for her "cocoon." But she wouldn't have said yes to Monte staying because his looks, his voice and especially his squatting down like that on his battered leg, with his painful back, to listen to Lily, had stirred her blood.

No. She would have said it because she was too tired to take them both on and then deal with Lily Rae's tears of persecution afterward.

Some days absolutely would just try the patience of a saint.

"Now," Lily said, from her spot halfway

between her mother and Monte, "have you all got your cocoons? Monte?"

"Yeah," he said. "Mine's right here."

She scuffled around.

"Monte? What are you doing? Are you putting on your nightgown?"

He chuckled. Jo Lena's heart turned over at the sound.

"No, I'm taking off my boots," he said. "I'm goin' to sleep in my clothes."

"I want to sleep in *my* clothes!"

From the sound, Lily Rae had sat up again.

Jo Lena threw her arm over her face. She could not deal with one more thing today.

Monte seemed to know that, too.

"Naw," he said. "You better stay in your nightgown, Lil."

"Why?"

"So that pink roan will know it's night and keep up her guard."

Lily seemed to think that over while Jo Lena was deciding that it didn't make much sense but it just might work.

"Lil," Lily Rae muttered to herself as she lay back down, "Monte calls me Lil."

Jo Lena smiled at that. Then a sudden thought stabbed her in the heart.

What would their lives have been like if Monte had never left the Hill Country?

These last six years would've been so different in nearly every way.

She pulled herself up short. Before he left, before all the bad things had happened, Monte hadn't asked her to marry him. They had both just assumed that it would happen someday. Maybe they wouldn't have even married.

But in her heart she knew that they would have. Back then, she and Monte had been made for each other. Everybody had seen that at a glance. Everybody had expected them to always be a couple.

Bits and pieces, pictures and images came floating into her mind. Picnicking with his whole family on the ranch at the waterfall bend of the Guadalupe River. She and Monte climbing a cliff at another spot on the river, talking about building a house there one day.

Monte hauling her and Annie to a cutting, parking the trailer in the shade.

Monte on a crooked-horned bull, her heart in her throat.

What was it he had said this morning?

I don't blame you for holding the past against me.

Monte finished with his boots and lay down. Lily Rae sighed once and began to breathe slow and deep.

114

"Monte?" Jo Lena said softly.

"Yeah?"

"You know what you said this morning about me holding the past against you?"

He was quiet for a long minute.

"What about it?"

His low voice was like a wind that just barely stirred the grasses. She could listen to it forever.

"I don't want you to think that," she said. "It's not true. I'm a lot stronger spiritually than I used to be and I want my life to show it."

He didn't answer for an age.

Finally he said, "What does that mean, Jo Lena?"

"That I want you and everyone else to see that I'm partnered with God to live every day He gives me to the fullest. That I know I shouldn't waste time and energy on grudges or regrets. So I don't."

The night suddenly seemed to stand still and wait for his answer. Then his voice came into the darkness and filled the space between them with so much pain she wanted to cry.

"Sounds good," he said.

Forlorn. He sounded forlorn, as if that could never be true for him.

"I have a million good memories to look

back on if I want to," she said, trying to take away some of his hurt. "All I *ever* held against you, Monte, was the way you left me."

She swallowed hard and bit back the sudden tears that threatened her.

"Because you don't know the whole story," he snapped.

Bitterly. Now he was bitter as well as hopeless.

"I think I probably do," she said gently. "Don't forget I'm the one person who knew you and Scotty both better than anybody else in the world."

He was silent forever.

"Right," he said at last. "Hold that thought."

Monte woke up still scared. He'd come so close to spilling his guts to Jo Lena last night that it was a miracle he hadn't lain awake for hours. He could thank his pain and exhaustion for that one lucky escape from his eternal regrets.

It might be true that he'd returned to the Hill Country to prove himself where it would mean something, but it was a fact that he had *not* come home to dredge up every shameful reason he'd gone away. Confessing everything to Jo Lena was not the way to go.

No, what he needed to do was keep his word and help her get those cookies made this morning.

He sat up.

But then he couldn't even reach for his boots.

There, on the far side of the pallet, was Jo Lena, sleeping all curled up around the pillow in her arms, with the first morning light reaching in through the window to make silver glints in her golden hair. He wanted to reach over there, brush it back from where it fell across her cheek. It lay free and loose in all directions over both her shoulders. She must've undone the braids when she went to bed.

He wanted to touch her flushed face and wake her, wanted to see the sleep fade from her eyes as she smiled at him.

Which was a dream. She'd probably wake, remember that she had no power and be furious with him all over again.

Lily Rae stirred, kicking against the tightness of her "cocoon," as she'd called it. She had managed to wind herself up in it until she could barely move.

Monte reached for his boots. He'd promised action on the electrical problem first crack out of the box, and he would make good on that. Surely he could find some fuses and get back by the time they woke up. It was barely daylight now.

Yet he pulled one boot on and then just sat there with the other in his hand. It was so different not to be waking up alone. For a long moment he just sat there, listening to the soft breathing of the child and the woman in the dawn dimness of the shadowed room.

Finally he stuffed his foot into his other boot, levered himself up and onto his feet by hanging on to the arm of the sofa, and walked as quietly as he could to the wall rack to get his hat.

"Monte," Lily Rae said slowly, "where are you going? Can I go with you?"

He turned to see her sitting up, rubbing her eyes sleepily. Jo Lena raised up on one elbow, pushing her hair back from her face, looking from Lily to him with a hazy stare.

"Monte?" she drawled, surprised, as if she'd forgotten he was there.

"I'm goin' after some fuses," he said very quietly, as if trying not to wake them completely. "I'll be back as quick as I can."

"Can I go?" Lily Rae asked.

Her voice quavered a little as if this one thing meant the world to her.

"Ask your mama," he said.

Jo Lena sat straight up and gained her senses.

"I have to put the butter out to soften," she said, and looked toward the kitchen. "I . . . no, I can't open the refrigerator . . . just in case . . ."

"Just in case of what?" Monte said.

"In case we can't get the power on very soon," she said. "It can hold the cold for twenty-four hours if we don't open it."

We.

"We'll get it on," he said, "you can trust me on that, Jo Lena."

She accepted that promise as innocently as Lily Rae would have and that warmed his heart.

"All right," she said, scrambling to her feet. "I'll put it out now. I've got to get those cookies started."

Padding barefoot across the room toward the kitchen, sleepily lifting her hair to hang down her back, she looked like the old Jo Lena. She might as well still have been in high school.

"Mama?" Lily Rae said. "Can I go with Monte?"

He couldn't resist taking a chance.

"Wash your faces, girls, and let's all go to Hugo's for breakfast. Then we'll go pick up our fuses. Don't y'all think it may be a little

119

too early to roust poor Old Man Donathan out of bed?"

"Ye-es! Ye-es! Ye-es!"

Lily Rae screamed with delight and ran out of the room, her shouts trailing along behind her.

"I'll put my clothes on!"

Jo Lena stopped stock-still and turned in the kitchen door to look at him. She didn't say anything.

Monte flashed her his most charming smile.

"Now, don't be calling me sneaky snake again," he said. "We all have to eat and you don't want to cook breakfast and then make twelve dozen cookies."

She was giving him a long, thoughtful look that really didn't tell him a thing. She might be furious, she might be thrilled — he couldn't tell.

I couldn't just walk out of here alone. Not after waking up in the same room with you. Don't you feel the same way, Jo Lena?

Maybe she did, maybe she didn't.

"*You* could cook," she said, and turned and went into the kitchen.

He followed her.

She went to the refrigerator, took the butter out and shut the door again.

"Can't keep it open *too* long," she said,

"since you're bound and determined — as always — to put pleasure before duty."

She started walking around the kitchen, pulling out big bowls and small bowls and long wooden spoons. When she went by the oven, she turned it on. They heard the small poof when it caught from the pilot light, the room was so quiet.

Anger roiled deep inside him.

"I told you you'd have electricity, and you will," he said. "It wouldn't hurt one thing for you to take out thirty minutes to eat your breakfast."

"I have a child to support and, for that reason, the reputation of my business to protect," she said tightly.

She was completely destroying the good mood he'd been in — the first one in a long while.

"And all I'm after here is to help you do exactly that," he snapped, trying to rein in his temper.

"Then take Lily to Hugo's — she likes their pancake sandwich — and then *go get that fuse, Monte.*"

He turned on his heel and walked out. He should've told Jo Lena his secret last night and then she wouldn't even be speaking to him this morning.

121

Chapter Six

But even if Jo Lena *was* speaking to him, he didn't have to do what she told him, did he? How had he wound up out here running around without her, taking care of her *child?*

Lily Rae had chattered nonstop since they'd left the house, making elaborate plans for future outings. Trips to the zoo in San Antonio to see the zebras. Horseback rides up onto the bluffs on the Rocking M with her on Annie. The rodeo at the county fair where he would ride a bull and she would barrel race on Annie.

All he was trying to do was get through breakfast, buy the fuse and take her safely home again.

What if she started crying? What if she had a temper fit or set her mind on doing something he couldn't permit? What if she did it anyway?

Jo Lena was the one who'd asked for the responsibility of Lily Rae and now she had shoved it off on him. He could tell her one thing: this wasn't going to happen again.

He would feed this child, find the right fuse, get the electricity flowing again to his entire ranch and then he'd keep close to his own house. Getting involved in other people's lives was always a huge mistake for him and he wasn't making it again.

When he pulled into the graveled parking lot at Hugo's, he heaved a huge sigh of relief. Only two other vehicles were out in front where the customers parked. He did *not* want to talk to a bunch of people and answer a million questions about life on the PBR circuit and try to be halfway sociable — which made him wonder all over again why he'd suggested eating out in the first place.

But what he *really* didn't want to talk to anyone about was his baby-sitting. Which would lead to questions about Jo Lena.

It was enough that everybody in the county would know before nightfall that he'd been seen buying breakfast for her child. Not to mention that he'd bought the place where she lived.

"Okay, Monte, can I unbuckle now?"

"Hold on a minute."

That was the main thing he should be relieved about, right there — he'd managed to arrive with Lily Rae still buckled into her seat belt, which was nothing short of a miracle, since she'd practically been bouncing off the doors and the ceiling the whole way. Jo Lena's ironclad command was that she was to stay in the back seat, belted. He also was not to let the child drink soda pop for breakfast and he was not to wait more than an hour before he called Mr. Donathan to open up and hunt for the fuse.

He sighed as he put the truck in park and shut off the engine. Nothing like taking orders from a woman when he wasn't even married.

"I'm going to help you decide what to eat, Monte," Lily said. "I've been here before."

He heard the ominous click as she freed herself from the restraint.

"Hold on I said. Give me a minute to help you out."

Last thing he needed was for her to go out the other door and step into the path of a moving vehicle. His anger at Jo Lena stirred again. There was no reason on earth she couldn't have come with them — except that she wanted to punish him for not getting an eighty-year-old man out of bed before good daylight. Didn't she realize they'd get much faster service if Old Man Donathan could be a little more rested? He was crotchety enough and plenty slow on his best day.

Monte opened his door, got out and un-latched the narrow back door on the driver's side.

"Come out this way," he said. "You have to stay right with me."

She was so excited she was smiling all over her eager little face. Irritated as he was, he couldn't help grinning back at her as he swung the door open.

In a way, if Jo Lena only knew it, this wasn't all punishment. Lily Rae really was pretty entertaining. She was a cute kid if a man could stand the aggravation.

"You can have more than one little pitcher of syrup if you don't waste it," she confided as she jumped down to the run-ning board and then to the ground.

"Great," he said. "I like plenty of syrup on my pancakes."

"So do I," she said. "Bunches."

She took his hand as a matter of course, which he hadn't expected, and they started toward the door. Her hand was impossibly small and trusting.

"The little pitchers are really cute," she said. "And they're plastic, not glass."

"Good," he said. "Then we won't break 'em when we squeeze out the very last drop."

She cocked her head and looked up at him

as they climbed the two shallow wood steps that led to Hugo's porch, crossed it and went inside.

"You can't squeeze 'em," she said.

She tried for the sure and certain tone she always used for her pronouncements, but her voice went up at the end of the sentence to make it a question. Monte grinned at her and shrugged.

"Have you ever tried?"

"No!" she cried happily.

She let go of him and began skipping down the aisle between the two rows of booths.

"Let's *do* it!" she crowed. "Let's squeeze the little pitchers!"

Hugo himself peered out of the pass-through to the kitchen and both waitresses turned to see who was coming in. Monte tried to look nonchalant.

"We're hungry for pancakes," he said. "Anybody here know how to make 'em?"

Lily skipped to a booth by the window and climbed up in the seat as one of the waitresses headed toward them.

"Wait 'til she can write it down," Lily said. "Hugo has to read it off the paper."

Then, as Monte accepted his menu and asked for black coffee, Lily said, "There's another Rocking M truck."

He glanced out at the parking lot and his heart dropped into his boots. Sure enough, she was right. Jackson in the passenger seat and Clint driving.

What rotten timing! That was absolutely all he needed. Nobody else, nobody, would give him a harder time about this.

He watched them park and get out. Wonderful. Now they'd be smirking and asking him again if he was still in love with Jo Lena.

Lily jumped down and came to climb up on the seat beside him.

"I'm sitting by you," she said. "They're not my brothers."

Sure enough, the minute they hit the door, they zeroed in on him. And then on Lily.

For a minute, they just stared as if they couldn't believe what they were seeing. They looked so surprised it was laughable.

The waitress followed Monte's glance and started laying two more places. His brothers both wore wide grins as they started toward him.

"Mornin'," Clint drawled, as they approached. "Can we sit here, or are we taking Jo Lena's seat?"

"You can sit," Lily said.

"Where is Jo Lena anyhow?" Clint said as

they slid into the opposite side of the booth.

Then he turned to Jackson.

"This must be a kidnapping, 'cause she knows ol' wild and woolly Monte can't take care of himself, much less a child."

It stung but it was about the truth. It made him mad, though, coming from perfectly responsible ol' Clint.

"That's a big brother for you," Monte said, with a sorrowful shake of his head. "Always trying to get a grip on everybody else's business."

"Mommy's not here. She's minding her *own* business," Lily Rae said, and they all laughed.

"What about you?" Jackson said, teasing her with a grin. "Are you minding your own business?"

"Yep, I'm helping Monte," she said with a decisive nod. "That's my business."

"What're you helping him do?" Jackson said lightly. "I never heard of Monte working."

"I'm helping him get his breakfast," Lily said. "He's going to eat pancakes."

"Can't he pick out his own breakfast?"

"No," Lily Rae said, unwrapping the napkin around Monte's silverware. " 'Cause he doesn't know how to act. He hollered through the window to Hugo."

"Well, how come you're out and about with such a rude, stinky old bull rider anyhow?" Jackson said.

She cut her eyes mischievously at Monte and grinned back at Jackson, wrinkling her small nose.

"His house is stinky, too," she said. "My mommy won't put her clean quilts on his floor."

Both brothers looked at him as that information soaked in.

"Your *house?*" Clint said.

"Yep," Monte said, pacified a little by the thought that for once, Clint hadn't known about something big before it happened. "Bought it yesterday."

They waited.

"Without telling any of us?" Clint said.

Monte shrugged.

"Figured it was none of your business."

"But he never bought any beds," Lily said. "That's why he had to sleep with me and Mommy in the dark last night."

She turned her big blue eyes to Monte and beamed at him fondly.

"It was fun, wasn't it, Monte?"

It would've been truly comical if it hadn't been so tragic. Jackson and Clint looked more dumbfounded than he had ever seen them. Monte had to laugh, in spite of all the misery he knew they were going to deal him later.

"Sure was," he said stoutly. "You just can't beat a good pallet on a clean floor."

Then he gritted his teeth while the waitress brought three coffees and a chocolate milk he hadn't known Lily ordered. Vaguely he wondered if chocolate milk was within the rules, but at the moment he didn't really care.

He felt like letting Lily drink all the soda pop she could hold. Every bit of this disaster was Jo Lena's fault.

"We-ell," Clint drawled, "reckon that might depend on who all is sharing that pallet, huh, Jackson?"

"That's what I'm thinking," Jackson said.

He, like Clint, was grinning from ear to ear.

"Which is nobody's business but mine," Monte said.

"Hmm," Jackson said, and made a great show of studying his menu. "So you bought the old Stoltz place."

He glanced up at Lily.

"Where *is* your mommy this morning, Lily Rae?"

"Making cookies," Lily said absently.

She was studying her straw, tearing its paper off across the end.

"She has to make twelve million thousand before two o'clock."

"How come y'all aren't helping her?" Clint said.

" 'Cause we have to get the fuse. But first we're getting pancakes!"

She held the glass in both hands and turned it up to drink half of it in one great gulp.

"Now, what do you McMahans all want to eat this morning?" the waitress said.

She raised her eyebrows when Lily ordered for herself and Monte, but he affirmed it with a nod and, while Jackson and Clint ordered, he frantically tried to think of a way to get his brothers off his back. He came up with nothing.

"So," Clint said, when the woman was gone, "y'all blew a fuse?"

"*Jo Lena* did," Monte said. "When I turned on the lights in *my* barn."

Maybe that would make it clear to the knuckleheads that he and Jo Lena were not living in the same house.

"The old Stoltz place," Jackson said thoughtfully, as if he still couldn't believe his ears about all this. "What kind of shape's it in now, Monte?"

"Electricity's not too stable," Monte said, and they all laughed.

Finally, they began recalling the times they used to hunt that ranch as boys, Lily Rae mercifully grew quiet, playing with the small packages of jam in their plastic carrier and Monte began to relax a little. Later, they would hoorah him about Jo Lena, that was true, but they were genuinely interested in his ranch and fascinated that he'd actually bought it. He had surprised them — a lot — and that tickled him.

The food came and, while they ate, the conversation mostly revolved around trying to squeeze the last drop of syrup from every little pitcher. But then, Clint pushed away his plate, leaned back and gave Monte his most irritating older-brother grin.

"It's hard to imagine," he drawled. "Monte fixing things. Taking care of things. Seeing after two houses and a barn and two other people."

"The *property* is my responsibility," Monte said.

Clint ignored that and shook his head doubtfully.

"You've always been the one breaking stuff, little bro," he said. "And I don't recall ever seeing you lift a hand at repairs in your whole life on the Rocking M. Better hire you some help. Go out and find yourself a crew this very mornin'. I can give you some

132

names if you want 'em."

Monte's stomach knotted again.

They had no faith in him. None. They didn't even see him as a grown man equal with them.

Until he proved them wrong, they would always think of him as the wild, irresponsible little brother who couldn't even maintain the place where he lived. The one who broke things and rarely finished what he started.

"Keep your names," Monte snapped. "I'm taking care of my own place."

"Never happen," Clint said. "You can't stay hooked up that long, Monte. We all know that."

"Yeah," Jackson said thoughtfully, "wonder how long it'll be 'til you put the old place up for sale again."

Monte's temper flared but he tried to hide it. He didn't want to give them the satisfaction of knowing they'd gotten to him.

"Well, I'm so full of surprises these days I even shock myself," he said, with a shrug. "Maybe y'all should just hide and watch me."

Jackson flashed an infuriating grin.

"Watch you fix up two houses and run a ranch while you baby-sit?"

Monte opened his mouth to say this was a

one-time deal, that he wouldn't be responsible for the little girl again. But then he felt Lily's big blue eyes on him.

He remembered the unfaltering trust of her small hand in his.

"You bet," he said. "You heard Lil. She's helping me."

He bit his tongue. How stupid could he be? Now Lily would be sure to stay right on his heels all the time. What had he been thinking? Hadn't he just promised himself to keep his distance from her and Jo Lena?

But then he turned to her and felt the full force of the smile she was beaming at him. Then she looked at Jackson and Clint.

"He calls me Lil," she said, her little face lit up like a candle.

Monte felt a new and surprising emotion swell his heart. This time, he was going to keep his word. He was not going to look into those innocent blue eyes and see that horrible, hurt disappointment like he'd caused in Jo Lena's.

As they left money on the table, though, and got up and went out to their trucks, he wasn't so sure he could do it. Honestly, deep down, he agreed with his brothers' assessment.

He'd never taken care of anything or anybody in his whole life and he doubted very much he could start now.

Jo Lena added the dry ingredients to the Butter-Nut Crunch batter and mixed until it was just moistened. Quickly, she began to shape it into tiny balls while she tried to shape her mind into some semblance of its usual self.

Not that her brain was usually the most organized in the world, but it was reasonably so. One thing was for certain — it hadn't been thinking about Monte for five long years now.

Until this morning. Until yesterday, when she had opened the door and he had walked through it into her refuge.

Until she had waked up to him in her house, her senses filling up wildly with the sound and the sight of him before she was half gone from sleep. The truth was that she probably didn't still love him — she most surely did not — but loving him once, a long time ago, might have spoiled her for ever loving any other man.

Monte had nearly killed her with heartbreak, and she mustn't forget that. But this morning he was making up for just one small portion of that misery by helping her out of this jam.

Which she would not be in if he hadn't caused it.

She clung to that thought, to that message from her little voice of truth. Monte meddling in her life was the reason she was beating all this batter by hand instead of using that time and energy to roll out and cut out the sugar cookies.

It was stupid to get all sentimental about him and remember how he looked so vulnerable with his black hair tousled from sleep that she had longed to run her hands through it. And to be grateful for his doing one errand — which she had not needed done until he blew her fuse — and getting breakfast for Lily. He owed her that kind of help and far, far more.

And it was stupid to be awash in the thoughts she'd been having while she worked: if it weren't for him, she would not have one batch of cookies made by now, much less three. She would've had to figure out what was wrong, go to get the fuse, see to Lily and her breakfast . . .

No. She must not, she *would* not get used to liking having him around, no matter how much he entertained Lily Rae and slept on her clean floors.

She must not let herself depend on him for anything.

Because Monte wouldn't stay. Here today, gone tomorrow, that was the famous wild bull rider, Monte McMahan.

She, of all people on the face of this earth, should know that best.

Jo Lena succeeded in dwelling on that truth until she finished all the cookies and delivered them to the library tea. She didn't let her thoughts get off course when Monte changed the fuse and then offered to take Lily Rae to Lupe's for her since he was going over to the Rocking M anyway, to talk to his mother and get a horse trailer and Annie.

She even held on to them when he stopped back by to see if she needed any more ingredients or if she'd need help transporting her wares to town. He had even volunteered to go put Annie up and come back to transfer the cooled cookies to boxes for carrying.

In spite of all that thoughtfulness, she had sent him straight home to his own house and put him entirely out of her mind. Almost.

But when she drove back onto the ranch from town, winding her way up to the cozy haven she'd created on the top of the hill there, her stubborn gaze stayed fixed on the big house set a hundred yards on the far side of her little one. Monte's house.

She tried it on her tongue.

"Monte's house."

That sounded so strange to her ears. Felt so weird to her tongue and her heart. All those years ago they had said "our" house when they talked about the future.

And now, here they were. There was Jo Lena's house. Over there was Monte's house.

And there was Monte.

Her heart jumped a little when she saw him.

He was riding Annie bareback, moving at a slow lope inside the old round pen that sat between their two houses. She watched them riding away from her, both of them looking completely relaxed and happy about what they were doing.

They had that air of contentment that came with doing nothing. Just sort of hanging out. Just letting things happen and going with the flow.

Which *she* hadn't done since she couldn't remember when.

The big old oak and sycamore trees scattered over the property threw enough shade that it dappled them, horse and rider, and when they came into the sun again it flashed on them and made them bright with color. Monte's cream straw hat and sky-blue shirt, his pale-blue faded jeans against the shining red sorrel of Annie's hide.

Annie moved with all her old grace and held her head and ears with all her old pride. The years hadn't changed that.

They came around on the other side, facing Jo Lena, and Monte saw her car. He lifted one hand in a casual wave but he dropped his eyes again and kept on riding, soft and serene, as if she wasn't there.

Jo Lena let her Explorer drift into the spot under the big sycamore by the gate in the front of her house and stopped it there instead of parking in her usual place at the side. She'd take a minute just to watch them some more before she picked up the mail from the seat beside her and went into the house to deal with it.

Plus she had to grate some carrots and make a carrot cake.

Monte and Annie kept going around and around, and her body leaned into their rhythm although she was sitting still. She hadn't taken time to ride Scooter over at the Rocking M since Monte came back.

And she hadn't ridden Annie since Monte brought her back into her life. It was the strangest thing that he'd been at the sale when Annie came through.

It was like God had deliberately put

Annie into Monte's hands to bring her horse back to her. Which obviously wasn't true, because he wasn't going to let her have her.

At least, not yet.

Next she'd be thinking God had done that to connect her with Monte again.

To banish that idea, she made herself move. She opened the door and got out of the car.

Annie nickered loudly.

Jo Lena looked up to see the mare looking straight at her, head up, ears pricked.

She called again.

Jo Lena smiled, let the door fall closed and started across the grassy space toward her old friend. The mail could wait. The cake could wait. She needed this.

She realized how *much* she needed it before she even reached the round pen. The tensions of the busy day soon left her as the sun soaked in and Monte and Annie continued their slow dance. They didn't stop until she opened the gate to the pen and went in and they had slow-loped around the circle to her again.

Annie muttered deep in her throat in a low, satisfied tone and nuzzled at her. Jo Lena reached up and hugged her around the neck.

When she drew back, she looked at Monte. His eyes met hers and held them. She couldn't read his thoughts at all, not one.

"Hey," he said.

"Hey."

Jo Lena stood still with the mare's cheek resting against hers. Monte leaned forward to stroke Annie's shoulder.

"How'd you two ever get separated in the first place?" he said.

"Money," she said with a shrug. "Just like everything else."

He was quiet for a minute.

"You had to have what she'd bring for . . ."

"Living, Monte. Just living. I had Lily and my dad's health problems to worry about. He had to quit working and it all just went on and on."

She saw the quick look of shock that passed through his eyes.

"Monte, my mother made a couple of really bad business deals right before she died," she said. "She even lost our place."

He frowned.

"Lily's got grandparents," he said. "How come the Kelleys weren't helping you?"

The old, cold chill struck her heart.

"I wouldn't let them. I still won't. I don't

141

want them to have any claim on her."

"Do they want any?"

She thought of the letter from their lawyer still lying, unopened, on the seat of her car.

"They've filed a custody suit."

He just looked at her, taking her in, taking in this information about her and putting it all together.

"After all this time?"

"She's nearly six now. They think they can take care of her now that she's not a baby anymore."

He thought about that.

Finally, he said, "Don't ever sell another horse you don't want to sell. Come to me instead."

The memory of those terrible days washed through her.

She looked at him straight.

"If I can find you."

He flinched, sort of an exaggerated parody of guilt. Then he flashed her that grin that always used to melt her right down to the ground.

"I'll be around," he said in a voice very low and sure.

Then he threw his leg over the mare and slid off, holding on to her withers until he landed carefully on the ground.

"Did you have as much trouble getting on

her as the first time?" she said.

He fixed her with a sharp, green gaze.

"How'd you know about that?"

"I saw you from the ridge. On my way back from the chapel."

He held the look for another long minute. Then he shook his head and grinned wryly.

"You always did see everything, Jo Lena."

She felt her mouth curve into a grin, too.

"You always did *do* everything, Monte."

"Life's short," he said lightly. "I was afraid I'd miss something."

She looked at him steadily.

"Well, did you?"

He looked back. For two long heartbeats.

"You know, Jo Lena," he drawled, "I'm beginning to think I did."

Chapter Seven

Jo Lena could barely get her mind around it: Monte thought he'd missed something by going away. Was that why he'd come back?

Little flashes of fantasy bombarded her. Monte reading the letter from the lawyer over her shoulder, Monte fixing up her house, Monte helping Lily Rae ride Annie, who was truly Jo Lena's horse. *Had* Monte bought this place because she was living here?

Had Monte come back to the Hill Country, not because he was hurt, but to find her again?

Monte McMahan, who never directly talked about his feelings — ever — had just admitted he'd missed a lot by leaving her. He had changed, he was different. . . .

And she was losing her mind.

She took a long, deep breath to try to slow the beating of her heart. Whatever Monte had missed was his own fault.

And *still,* after six years, he was thinking only of himself. Of what *he* had missed.

What he had *missed* was being at her side when she needed him most. It still made her sad and it made her mad to think about it.

"Really?" she said. "What is it you think you've missed, Monte?"

His look was so intense, so searching, that it stirred her heart. She began to lose the anger.

"Sudden blackouts, for one thing," he drawled, grinning at her while he absently stroked Annie's neck.

"You didn't miss any of those. We never had them until you came back."

"I missed dozens of cinnanmum cookies," he said.

"True."

"And I missed waking up on your clean floor . . ."

"True."

". . . and seeing you open your big, blue eyes to the new morning."

She stared at him as her heart turned over. He had felt the same subtle magic she had felt, there in her big, shadowy living room, when the sun came up.

He took off his hat and then resettled it on his head, his warm green gaze never leaving hers. His hair was tousled. She wanted to brush it off his forehead and smooth it to the side.

"You must be thinking about Lily Rae," she said. "She has big, blue eyes."

"True," he said, "but it's you I'm thinking about, Jo Lena."

She wanted to flirt back, she wanted to turn and walk away, she wanted to tell him he was six years too late with that smile, she wanted to take two steps and walk into his arms. She had to get out of here this minute.

I'll be around.

He had said that in the surest tone possible.

But he wouldn't be. Before very many days had passed, he'd be oblivious to anything he might've missed right here at home and be off chasing after some other life experience that he was afraid to lose.

This was Monte McMahan and she'd better not forget it.

She couldn't forget it. There had never been another man like him in her life and, suddenly, with a knowledge that speared her in the heart, she knew there never would be another one like him for her.

I'll be around.

Could it be that God had sent him back to her to stay?

Her blood leapt, singing, through her veins. She had to lean on Annie to prop up her knees and keep her legs under her.

146

Monte just stood there smiling softly, looking at her as if he didn't intend to do another thing for the rest of the day.

"Want to ride her?" he said lazily.

She didn't want to move a single muscle, either. She couldn't think of a reason to.

"Oh," she said, "mostly I just want to be with her."

And with you. Mostly I just want to be with you.

The dappled sunshine fell across them, moving back and forth a little with the wind moving in the trees. Music came and went on the breeze, the sweet, upbeat melody drifting out to them from the barn.

They were the old Monte and Jo Lena, unhurried and young and innocent of all that would pass between them. Then that thought was gone, too, and there was only this sunlit moment to live.

"Annie's a fine loper," he said. "Good enough for a pleasure horse."

"Or for a broodmare," she said.

His eyes crinkled at the corners when his smile broadened. Those fine lines there proved this wasn't the old Monte.

"What'd I tell you?" he said. "You haven't changed a bit. You still see everything."

You haven't changed a bit.

147

Her dormant mind stirred vaguely. When it came to Monte, she *had* changed. Hadn't she?

"Who's the daddy?"

"Sunny Meridian."

"Sounds good," she said.

But she'd lost the thread of what they were talking about. She couldn't quite remember what question she'd asked. Monte's eyes were very green and clear. They held the same faint smile that hovered around his mouth.

He was looking at her as if she were the only other person in the whole world. The melody, high and happy, sang to them without words and then it was gone again, carried on the vagaries of the wind.

"So," she said, "I hear you've got your music hooked up."

"Strictly battery powered," he said. "Not to be blamed for our recent electrical outage."

Our.

Why was it that every time he used that word — or *we* or *us* — it gave her such a warm feeling?

It made her want to touch him, every time. Right now it sent a longing through her to reach out and trace her fingertips over his face.

His familiar face, which was handsome beyond belief, called to her to touch it. She would cup his cheek and run her thumb along his high cheekbone. She'd trace the line of his jaw with it, too.

His face was some different — it had grown harder as he grew older. Even now, in spite of his smile, the hardness was still on him. These last six years hadn't been easy for him, either.

It took all her determination, but she made fists of both hands and dug her short nails into her palms so she'd wake up from this dream and face reality. Finally, when she felt more in control, she made herself reach for Annie's halter.

"Maybe we should rinse her off," she said. "She's worked up a sweat."

"So have I," Monte said.

Jo Lena turned and led the mare toward the unlatched gate.

"Then let's rinse you off, too," she said.

"That could be interpreted as an invitation to a water fight," Monte said, "but I'll overlook it this time since you're all dressed up and looking so pretty."

Jo Lena risked one quick glance over her shoulder.

"You haven't changed a bit, either," she said. "Always full of baloney."

149

He pretended to be hurt.

"Would I lie to you?"

"It is a distinct possibility."

"Jo Lena," he drawled, "you're a hard girl."

"I just tell it like it is."

He walked faster, coming up closer behind her. His leg must be getting much better.

"I never lied to you," he said. "That's one thing in my favor and you have to admit it."

He was right beside her when she led Annie up to the outdoor faucet by the barn and tied her to the hitching post. Jo Lena didn't look at him. And she wasn't going to answer him, either. Talking about the past would only ruin this beautiful day.

And besides, if he hadn't lied, he certainly hadn't always been honest with her.

"If I had a hose attached to this faucet," she said, "I'd rinse off this mare."

"Think about it while I'm gone," he said as he went on into the barn for the hose. "You can't dispute that I'm right."

She patted Annie's pretty neck and stood back to look at her profile.

"You're still the prettiest mare of all, pregnant or no," she said. "And your baby's going to be gorgeous, too."

It helped to fix her mind on this favorite

horse of hers and the future foal. It helped to look up into the wide, blue sky and let the breeze play in her hair that she'd worn loose to go into town. It helped to listen to the music coming from the barn, the new song with the lilting rhythm and its story about runaway lovers.

Monte had run away without her, all that long time ago.

Now, Monte hadn't come back to stay. It wasn't in his nature. She knew him well.

He came out of the barn carrying the hose.

"How far along is Annie?" she said.

"Don't try to change the subject," he said. "Did I ever lie to you?"

"Yes," she said firmly, "you did. You *behaved* a lie, Monte, more than once."

He bent over to fit the end of the hose onto the faucet.

"But did I ever tell you a lie in so many words?"

"You are the stubbornest man I ever met in my life!" she cried.

He turned on the water, straightened up and started uncoiling the hose as he walked toward her.

"*Did* I?"

"*No!* Not that I can remember. And believe me, I'm trying!"

"Well, then," he said, as if he'd won a significant argument.

He handed her the nozzle, they both reached to twist it on at the same time and his hand, big and rough and warm, closed over hers. Jo Lena felt a trembling thrill go up through her arm.

Which was totally ridiculous.

"So what?" she said. "So what if I can't think of a lie you *told* me?"

She thought she would pull her hand away but she didn't.

"It proves I *didn't* ever lie to you. Not only do you see everything, you remember everything, too."

He let her hand go, then, and took a step back to stand beside her. It felt so right for him to be exactly there. It felt so wrong for him not to be touching her.

She gave him a sideways, teasing glance.

"Are you comparing me to the elephant who never forgets?" she said.

He shrugged.

"You said it. I didn't. Remember that, too."

They looked at each other for a long minute, while the matching, slow grins grew on their faces. Some things never changed.

How many times had they shared this look? How many times had this easy feeling lay between them during all the long days they'd gone everywhere together and thought that was the way things would always be?

Things never stayed the same. Everything always changed.

Jo Lena turned away and started spraying water on Annie's lower legs, testing her out by gradually going higher and higher. The mare stood still as ever, totally unperturbed.

"Thank goodness," she murmured, "nobody scared her while she was gone."

"And now she's back," he said.

"With you," she said, as much to herself as to him. "Not with me."

"We both live on the same place in case you haven't noticed," he said. "She's with *us* now, Jo Lena."

The warm thrill ran through her again. Why did he keep saying things like that?

Lord, did You send him here on purpose? You must have, to have sent Annie with him. What do You want me to do with him?

"Monte," she said, "what difference does it make now whether you ever told me a lie all those years ago or whether I remember it? Why did you bring that up?"

She let the water play over Annie's withers, watched it run over her back, shining sorrel in the sun. For a long minute,

153

she thought he wasn't going to answer.

Finally, she glanced at him.

"Because I want you to see one good thing about me."

He was trying for a light, carefree tone but the pain in his voice was a palpable thing. It broke her heart.

"Oh, Monte!"

Jo Lena whipped around to look at him full face. She let the water just run out onto the ground while she searched his eyes and his soul.

She found the hurt there, too. It went so deep, she couldn't look away from it. She couldn't move. It held her stock-still.

"There are *lots* of good things about you!"

He didn't believe her — because he didn't see any good in himself. That was as plain on his face as if he'd spoken the words.

"There's another thing that hasn't changed about you, Jo Lena. You always say something kind to everyone."

"I mean it," she said. "Monte, don't you believe me?"

He only looked at her. She had never seen such misery.

He absolutely knew that he could trust her, yet he would not let himself take comfort from her. Hadn't she told him last night that she wasn't holding a grudge? Was he punishing himself this much?

"*You're* kind, too," she said. "Look at how you treat Lily Rae, and Annie! And me!"

He shook his head hopelessly.

"Have *I* ever lied to *you?*" she cried.

"You're such an innocent, Jo," he said sarcastically. "You don't know a scumbag when you see one."

Fury raced through her. Absolute fury.

"Don't you call yourself names! Don't you *dare!* God loves you, and your mother loves you, and your sisters and brothers love you, and Lily Rae loves you and I . . ."

Fortunately, she bit her lip before she said it. She threw the hose down and turned to get out of there before she did herself in, but he caught her hand as she whirled away from him and pulled her into a kiss that shocked her right down to the ground.

His mouth took hers and stopped her breath, stopped her heart beating, stopped the anger in her blood and her mind in its chaos. Everything else went away. Six long, hard years went away.

After that first, desperate demand, Monte kissed her like he used to kiss her, with his whole heart and soul and all the time in the world. His lips felt so warm, so good, so *familiar.* They remembered hers.

155

And her lips remembered his. They definitely remembered his.

She breathed in the scent of him, which was familiar, too. It was made up of horse and sweat and leather, yes, but also it held the magical, individual smell that was Monte, only Monte.

Her heart started up again and racketed in her chest like a wild thing in a trap. Her arms lifted and wrapped themselves around his neck without any direction from her. She tilted her head and sincerely began to kiss him back.

All she'd been needing all this long time was Monte.

But that started her mind up again, too. It began screaming like a door on rusty hinges.

She'd better *not* be needing Monte. Monte wouldn't stay. She might fall in love all over again and then Monte would be gone.

Jo Lena broke the kiss as brusquely as he'd started it.

Instinctively, Monte tried to hold her for a moment, but she dropped her arms away from his neck and pushed to be free and he let her go. She took a quick step back and turned away, her head down and her long hair swinging across her face.

It made him feel alone and lonesome and

he reached for her again before he could stop himself. He was glad she had her back to him and didn't see.

"I'm sorry, Jo Lena," he said, "I had no right to kiss you."

What was *wrong* with him? He'd been so full of self-loathing one minute that he couldn't even accept a nice word from her, and the very next minute he'd grabbed her and kissed her. He was going over the edge.

All morning he'd been feeling halfway contented or relaxed like that for the first time in six years. Now he'd ruined it all.

"I'm sorry," he said again. "I gave up every right to kiss you a long time ago."

"*I* kissed *you,* too," she said. "I shouldn't have done that. I guess I'm just extravulnerable today."

Monte's heart gave a painful thump.

She already had enough trouble without adding him into the mix. For her sake, he needed to stay as far away from her as possible and still live on the same property.

He needed to do that for his own sake, too. He could never be a good enough man to deserve her.

When he started listening again, she was saying, "So you see, you can't claim *all* the guilt."

She went to the hose and picked it up,

smooched to Annie and pushed her hip around so she could rinse off her side.

He had to lighten things up. The only way for them to coexist on this ranch was to keep it light.

"All *right,* then," he said. "I'll lay half the guilt on you."

She pushed her hair back on one side and he saw that his mocking tone had made her smile a little.

"All *right,* then," she said, mocking him in return.

Then she lifted her head and looked straight at him over Annie's back.

"I'm sorry, Monte," she said in her old, direct way. "Don't go into another funk thinking I didn't want to kiss you. That's not it."

"Then what is it?"

"I *wanted* to kiss you — that's what."

She dropped her eyes to watch the water run into Annie's mane.

Those words made his blood beat a little faster. He walked over to the door of the barn, picked up the comb he'd left on the barrel and used it as an excuse to go to her.

"So that's a bad thing, wanting to kiss me?" he said.

"There you go again, feeling all guilty," she said.

He started combing the mare's wet mane.

"Kissing you is a bad thing because I mustn't risk getting attached to you again," she said.

"Well, I can certainly understand why you feel that way," he said reasonably. "The last time you did it . . ."

"Now don't start beating yourself up all over again," she said sharply. "I mean I can't be getting attached to any man."

A weird stab of disappointment got him.

"I don't know how 'any man' got into this," he said. "I was the one kissing you."

She tossed back her hair and laughed at him. Her husky chuckle made him want to kiss her again, more than he wanted to stroke the silk of her hair.

"You sound like a little boy pouting," she said. "What I'm saying is that I'm not going to get involved with any man and start depending on him. I'll depend on God and myself and that's all."

He thought about that. *This* was his doing, too. Now she'd not only never trust him again, but she'd never trust any other man, either. The way he had left her had caused her to feel this way.

New guilt clutched at him.

"Sounds sorta narrow-minded to me," he said. "Maybe you oughtta rethink that."

"Nope," she said, and went to turn off the water.

"You're judging every man in the world by me," he said, making himself come out with the truth.

Jo Lena turned and gave him a glance he couldn't read.

"Don't do that, Jo. I don't want to be responsible . . ."

"For what?"

"For . . . if you never marry. . . ."

Monte started working a tangle out of Annie's long, flaxen mane. He had done all the soul-baring he could do for now — probably for the rest of his life.

Jo Lena walked up to the other side of Annie and started scraping the water off her hide.

"Monte, are you telling me you want me to get married?"

He looked at her in alarm.

"No! No, I . . . that's your business, Jo Lena. It's none of mine."

She gave her husky laugh.

"Well, thank goodness," she said. "There for a minute, I thought —"

Monte didn't let her finish. He couldn't, because he had to know.

"What did you mean when you said that you're extravulnerable today, Jo Lena?"

"That's the *only* reason I kissed you back," she said quickly.

Too quickly. He smiled to himself. That was a good sign.

No, wait. It was a bad sign. They could never get back together.

"*What* were you talking about?"

"I got another letter from the Kelleys' lawyer," she said. "I'm afraid to open it because there's no way I can afford to hire an attorney of my own, and my car payment's coming up, and the rent's due."

He tried to sort all that out.

"Therefore," he said slowly, "you must not kiss or get attached in any way to any man who might be able to front you a little money or give you some advice and comfort?"

"Right," she said, nodding as if that were the most sensible statement in the world. "If I depend on someone else and then he lets me down, I might lose everything. It's better for me to be prepared and know what my limits are."

"Even if you can't afford a lawyer?"

"Yes," she said, but she didn't sound quite so certain anymore.

"I'm not sure that makes a whole lot of sense," he said slowly, trying not to antagonize her.

"It does to me. I have to know where I

stand at all times for Lily Rae's sake. I can't have her future depending on somebody else."

"Well, not just anyone," he said.

She eyed him narrowly.

"I know what you're thinking," she said.

"For starters, forget the rent," he said.

She leaned on her clenched fists, which she propped on Annie's rump.

"Don't start," she said. "I should never have told you."

He flashed her a glance.

"But you had to, remember?" he said. "I might've loathed myself to death if you hadn't explained why you broke off the kiss like that."

It made her laugh, as he'd intended.

"Right. But don't insult me by trying to give me money."

"I'm not," he said. "I'm just saying I won't take your money."

She stood up very straight.

"You have to," she said. "Or I'll move and Lily Rae will die of pining for you, and my business will tank because I won't have a good, big kitchen anymore."

"Pay me in cinnanmum products," he said. "Of any description. And I'm partial to biscuits and cornbread and yeast rolls by the dozen."

She frowned at him.

"No. Man cannot live by bread alone," she said.

"I like steak and potatoes and turnip greens and pinto beans, and Mexican and Italian food, too."

She just looked at him. She was looking downright interested. He wouldn't push it.

Oh, well, yes, he would. It was such a great idea that had just come to him.

"If I could eat even one meal a day at your house, Jo Lena, that'd be worth the world to me. I am so sick of eating out that I'm ready to starve first."

She looked shocked. And sympathetic, if he wasn't reading her wrong.

"You see how thin I am," he said.

Food was always the ticket with Jo Lena. Feeding hungry people gave her great pleasure. And she loved to cook. That was just like his mom — they both had always claimed that anything they cooked was better than what could be found in any restaurant.

"I'm sorry, Monte," she said sincerely. "I know you crave home cooking."

"I'd sure rather have that than rent money," he said.

He started to add that he hadn't had any home cooking for six years, but then he decided he really shouldn't go there. Not now.

"You could cook for yourself," she said. "I could tell you how."

"I won't have time," he said. "And you're far too busy with your business to be giving me cooking lessons."

Her blue eyes smiled at him.

"And what will be keeping *you* so busy?"

He tried to think fast.

"Repairs," he said. "I'm going to start restoring the big house."

He hadn't even considered it until that very minute.

"Chris's nephew said the place ought to be on the National Register of Historic Places," he said, as if that explained everything.

Her eyes had gone wide.

"That's my *dream*," she said, heedlessly clasping the scraper to her chest.

Dirty water ran down the front of her blouse and she didn't even notice.

"Ever since I moved here I've dreamed of somehow getting a loan to buy this ranch and restore that house. Then I'd turn it into the most wonderful bed-and-breakfast in all of Texas."

A strange glow took hold of his heart.

"Great idea," he said, nodding briskly. "If you pay me in food, you can put your rent money toward the down payment."

She cocked her head and looked at him narrowly.

"You won't sell me my horse, so I can't see you selling me this ranch."

"I'm an unpredictable man, Jo Lena."

She raised her eyebrows and gave him a look.

"As *I* know far better than anyone else on the face of the earth," she said. "But I also know that I can depend on you to show up at mealtime and put your feet under the table. So, if you're serious about that offer you just made, we've got a deal."

Monte stuck out his hand.

"Deal," he said. "My mouth's watering already."

"Deal," she said. "I'm headed for my kitchen. After doing business with you, I need the therapy."

Her hand felt small and soft in his but he could feel the calluses on her palm. Probably from wielding that long, wooden stirring spoon.

A current seemed to flow from her skin to his. He couldn't quite bring himself to turn loose of her.

"At supper let's talk about my buddy the lawyer," he said.

She gave him that narrow-eyed threatening look he remembered so well.

"We've made a trade for my rent," she said. "But I have nothing else to barter. No way are you going to pay for me to have a lawyer."

He let go of her hand and raised both of his, palms out, in defense.

"No money involved," he said. "This guy owes me big-time. I'd be calling in a marker, that's all."

"And then *I'd* owe *you* big-time," she said.

"Totally impossible," he said seriously. "I already owe you this and much, much more, Jo Lena."

She looked shocked and then hurt.

"Well, thanks a *lot*, Monte McMahan!"

"*What?* What'd I say?"

Tears appeared in her eyes.

"Nothing."

She bit her lip. Her luscious, full lower lip, which he would really like to kiss again.

"I just didn't know that was why you wanted to help me, that's all."

"What? Why did you think?"

The tears threatened to spill.

"I just wasn't thinking of all this bargaining in terms of *debts* to one another."

Exasperation took him over.

"Good grief, Jo Lena, we were talking

166

about you owing me *rent!* Isn't that talking about debts?"

She turned away.

He followed her.

"Why did you think I wanted to help you, Jo?" he said softly.

"I — I wanted it to be because you . . ." She stopped and swallowed hard. "Just because you . . . like me. Because we're still . . . friends. I thought."

With a wanting that flooded every muscle in his body, he longed to take her into his arms.

Surprise filled him, too, for he hadn't known that she needed comfort as much as he did.

"I do like you, Jo Lena," he said quietly. "I'll never stop . . . liking you."

She brushed away her tears and he let her do it. He would not touch her anymore, no matter how much he wanted to.

Chapter Eight

Monte cut two thick slices from the loaf of pumpernickel bread that Jo Lena had sent home with him and buttered them to eat while the potatoes browned in the skillet that came from a box of kitchen stuff his mom had thrown together for him. He beat some eggs in a bowl. He couldn't believe how hungry he was, now that Jo Lena had whetted his appetite. One good supper at her house and here he was, cooking breakfast for himself.

It felt so strange. Food hadn't even been a blip on his radar screen for all these years while he was on the road. He'd eaten only for fuel and hadn't cared what it was or how much of it there was until he'd finally reached the point that he didn't care whether or not he ate anything at all.

He took a big bite of the sour bread and sweet butter to ease his growling stomach, picked up the fork and started beating the eggs. They looked just like his mind had felt after Jo Lena scrambled it yesterday.

It could've been one of those twisted Swedish pretzels by the time she got done worrying about one thing and then another, and thinking one way and then the opposite way, and then jumping from wanting to be completely independent to wanting him to offer help. And it had to be for the right reason, too: not because he owed her but because he liked her.

Wasn't that just like a woman?

Here she'd been acting all along as if she didn't want so much as to see his face.

He whistled a little tune as he poured the eggs on top of the potatoes and started stirring them all together in the sizzling skillet. This was just simple campfire cooking but he must make sure not to mention it to Jo Lena. He didn't want her to think he was able to feed himself in any way.

When the eggs were done, he sat down at the rickety table that had probably stood in this kitchen since the flood, and looked around the room while he ate. A bed-and-breakfast, huh?

Well, it would need a dishwasher. And a bigger stove. There was room for a huge one where this old two-burner one was and space for a double-wide refrigerator over in the corner. No telling what else would have to be done.

All the electrical wiring, and all the plumbing would probably have to be replaced. This house would have to be taken down to the studs. Plus, to be registered as an historic place, every single thing would have to be done according to some greatly detailed rules, no doubt.

He sighed. He'd shot off his mouth about restoring this place when he had no clue what he was talking about.

A little surge of excitement went through him, though. It was so weird that the project he'd hit upon right off the top of his head turned out to be Jo Lena's secret dream. That seemed almost as if it were meant to be.

A small voice spoke somewhere in the back of his mind. Could it be that God had given him this opportunity to do something good for Jo Lena to make up just a part of all the wrong he'd done her?

He pushed the thought away and focused his attention on the real world again. God had no use for him or He would've saved Scotty's life that night.

Monte made himself look around the huge kitchen. He'd thought when he bought the place that he could never live anywhere permanently and then he'd known that he could never sell it when he found Jo Lena on the property. So here it was, or soon would be: her bed-and-breakfast, her dream come true.

Once, long ago, her dream had been a home with him.

But he wouldn't let himself think about that, either. Jo Lena had no more use for him than God did.

He would simply concentrate on what needed to be done to restore the place and he wouldn't just hire someone to do it, either. He'd told Jo Lena that's what would be keeping him busy and no way was he breaking his word to her, whether the work turned out to be boring or not.

Honestly, he didn't have anything else to do. Working on this house was bound to teach him a lot of skills and it'd certainly be new and different, which was what he was always after, wasn't it?

Who knew? Maybe he'd go into historic restoration if he couldn't ride bulls anymore.

A pang of regret hit him hard as he ate the last bite of his eggs and potatoes. If he couldn't ride bulls or broncs anymore, what *would* he do for excitement? He had to have a challenge, he needed that always-thrilling rush of adrenaline to make him feel alive. He'd lived for that since he was knee-high to a grasshopper.

Resolutely, he pushed back from the table. All he could do was work with what strength and flexibility he had right now and hope for the best. The early-morning stretches he'd started today seemed to have helped. Soon he would try really working out again.

Right now, he had to focus on something else. He would drive into San Antonio and learn what he needed to know about historic restoration while he hoped like crazy that his back would heal fast and heal enough for him to ride again. His leg was much better. Surely he wasn't out of the game for good.

The front door flew open and slapped the wall.

"Mo-nte!"

That was Delia's voice.

"Hey, Monte, up and at 'em! Let's get this place whipped into shape and I mean *now!*"

And that was LydaAnn's.

Quick, hot anger surged into his blood. Couldn't they give him some privacy in his own house?

And some respect? Nobody in the whole family thought he had an ounce of responsibility in him and now, evidently, they'd decided he couldn't even clean his own house.

He left his plate on the table and went to throw the meddlers out.

But there they were, his baby sisters, looking and acting as if they were teenagers again. Delia and LydaAnn were stubbornly trying to struggle through the doorway at the same time, both with armfuls of mops, brooms, buckets and cleaning supplies. Even a shovel. In spite of himself, he grinned.

They looked hilarious. They wore bandannas tied down over their hair, tool belts stuffed with dust cloths, spray cleaners and brushes strapped around their waists, and T-shirts that read Hill Country Clean Team — We Sweep Your Floors, Stomp Your Bugs, and Sing While We Do It.

Monte shook his head and tried not to laugh because that would only encourage them.

But he still couldn't quit grinning. Obviously, they hadn't lost their will to go to any lengths for one of their silly scenarios. They hadn't changed a bit since they were little girls putting on plays for audiences that ranged from their playmates to the whole family to everyone living on the ranch.

"So why is everyone always picking on *me* as the McMahan who will never grow up?" he said.

They stuck out their tongues and rolled their eyes at him in answer and then, as soon as they got through the door, they struck a pose and began to sing in their tight, sisterly harmony:

"If dirt's knee-deep in your living room and trash piled high on your set-tee, we'll shovel it out and haul it off and that we will guar-an-tee, if you'll smile and hang tight with our Hill Country Clean Team we'll do all your work, take away all your troubles and make your sad face beam!"

They sang the last line a little too fast, to make it fit, then hummed a little riff of an ending and stood there smiling at him expectantly.

Monte tried, he really tried, but he could not hold back a laugh.

They had gone to a lot of trouble for him. They must truly be glad he was back because usually even Bobbie Ann couldn't get them to do housework of any kind.

"I knew I should've put locks on this house before I carried in my gear bag," he said.

"That's no way to talk to the unpaid help," LydaAnn said, laughing back at him. "You'll be changing your tune by the end of the day, Monte McMahan, when you see what we all can do to this filthy rat hole."

"I like it just the way it is."

"You haven't seen it clean for comparison," Delia said, trying for her most authoritative tone.

She was laughing, too, though. At the expression on his face, no doubt.

"What's this 'end of the day' and 'we all can do' business?" he said.

"The whole family's coming," LydaAnn said as she abandoned her tools and started exploring the room. "Jo Lena's cooking supper for everybody and Ma's bringing snacks to get us by 'til then."

They were even horning in on his supper with Jo Lena.

Which was good, come to think of it. He didn't need to be getting attached to any rituals with Jo Lena.

But the whole family! Here for the whole day!

"Give me a break," he said. "Call the others off. It'll take me all morning to run off just the two of you."

"Longer than that," Delia said. "We want to look the place over and see what all you'll have to do to restore it."

A quick stab of annoyance and something else — jealousy or betrayal — ran through him. That had been a private conversation between him and Jo Lena. This was their deal and Jo didn't need to be talking to anybody else about it.

"What *is* this?" he demanded. "Jo Lena must've been on the phone all night telling everything she knows."

"Nope, it was Lily Rae," LydaAnn said. "She and Maria and Lupe helped us gather up our supplies."

"That little rascal," Monte grumbled. "First she tells Clint and Jackson my floors are dirty, and now this."

"Yep," Delia said. "But don't you say a word to her. She's our best source of information and I don't know what we'd do without her."

"What y'all might do is mind your own business," Monte said. "I'm telling the kid to zip her lip."

"No way," LydaAnn said. "It'd break her heart. If she thought she'd displeased her wonderful Monte, she'd never get over it."

He was fast losing his sense of lightheartedness. One reason was this sisterly invasion but another was that he'd just recognized that his desire for a project or some connection that included only him and Jo Lena ran really deep.

That line of thinking was a definite slippery slope. He had better welcome everyone

176

he could find to make a crowd between him and Jo.

Yet he couldn't resist trying one more time.

"Look, girls," he said. "Let's forget this for now, because I was just on my way into San Antonio. I'll hire a crew some other day."

Delia was examining the details of the window moldings.

"No, Monte, you can't," she said absently. "Mom's looking forward to the whole family being together for the day and you've broken her heart enough times in six years. Nothin' for it but to sit still and take your medicine today, big bro."

Then she turned and gave him a look that showed she wasn't quite so absentminded, after all.

His old guilt stirred to stronger life inside him. The irritation flared again, too, but he might as well get a grip on it because Delia was right. This day of mothering him and cleaning up his house would mean the world to Bobbie Ann, and he'd already disappointed her by coming home to the Rocking M and then leaving it again so soon.

Another vehicle pulled up into the yard and honked a greeting. It was one of the four-door ranch pickups hauling a two-horse trailer — Monte saw it through the window.

"Y'all must really think this place is dirty," he said. "Looks like Clint's brought a whole trailerload of cleaning supplies."

"Maybe the trailer's to haul off the trash," Delia said.

His sisters came to give him hugs.

"You can stand it, sweetie," LydaAnn said. "Just this one day and then we'll all leave you alone. Maybe."

Monte shook his head woefully.

"I went out and bought a whole ranch trying to escape from these early-morning visits," he said, hugging them back, one in each arm. "Spent over a million dollars and it didn't do me a dime's worth of good."

"You went at it all wrong," Delia said. "If you'd split the million between us in bribes, that might've done the trick."

"It would not," LydaAnn said. "This is much more fun than spending money."

Monte groaned.

"If that's the way y'all feel, then I'm in trouble deep," he said.

"You got it," they said in chorus.

"Darcy! You and Cait come here and look," Bobbie Ann yelled from the front porch, "we've got our work cut out for us.

This house hasn't been cleaned for years."

Monte turned to see his mother peering in through the ragged screen door. She grinned at him over the stack of food containers she was balancing in both arms.

"I may have to stay with you all next week, son, just to finish up sanitizing the whole place. This looks like a real challenge."

She had a little chortle in her voice. She was enjoying this as much as his sisters were. Now they were both laughing at him again.

"Stay as long as you want, Ma," he said perversely. "I'd love to have the company."

LydaAnn elbowed him in the side.

"Well, thanks a lot!" she said. "Ma, he was trying to throw *us* out but he said *you* can stay."

"I'm so sorry, sugar," Bobbie Ann said with exaggerated kindness. "But that's because he knows he can trust *me* not to sing."

That made LydaAnn and Delia start singing again and Monte dragged them both toward the door. Wrestling and arguing as if they were all kids again, they worked their way toward the porch to help Bobbie Ann with the load of food she'd brought.

"You do have refrigeration, don't you,

Monte?" she said.

"Yeah, but it's an old machine. I doubt it'll hold all of this."

"If not, Jo Lena said she had some room."

Monte took some of the big plastic boxes she held.

"Jo Lena's in trouble," he said darkly. "She should've warned me about this little party."

"We asked her not to tell," Bobbie Ann said, "for fear you'd run away and not be here to do your part."

Monte turned to lead the way into the house as his brothers and both sisters-in-law piled out of the truck.

"My part is supervisory," he said.

"In your dreams," Delia said.

That reduced him to pleading.

"Come *on*, Ma," he said desperately. "What's the point of cleaning this house when we'll just have to tear out the walls and ceilings to renovate the place?"

"Are you going to be living here while all that's going on?" Bobbie Ann demanded.

"Yes."

"Well, then. *That's* the point."

They all laughed.

"Easy to see you've been gone too long, Monte," Delia said. "You've forgotten how the world works."

Clint called from the yard.

"Hey, Monte, hold on. Jackson and I are gonna rescue you from these women. Get yourself on out here."

The four of them stopped and let the screen door fall closed again. Cait and Darcy were climbing the porch steps. Clint and Jackson were both going back to look in on whatever they had in the trailer.

"Only for a little while!" Bobbie Ann called back to him. "Clint, do you hear me? Go straight to the sale, drop the horse off and come directly back here."

Monte handed his boxes of food to Delia and started toward the steps to go look at the horse, too.

"What time is supper?" Clint said, teasing his mother.

"Y'all better not be gone *that* long," Bobbie Ann said darkly. "Lupe's bringing Maegan and Lily Rae to us at noon and y'all have to baby-sit."

Clint grinned and waved at her as he turned to look at the horse again. Monte joined him.

"Who's this going to the sale?" he said.

"A truly ornery beast we call Cactus for his disposition," Jackson said. "He's a Gold Chocolate, bred for Western Pleasure, but nobody can stay on him."

"A slight detriment for a show horse," Monte said dryly.

"Exactly," Clint said. "He's outta here before he hurts somebody. I'm tired of fooling with him."

"Pretty head," Monte said, as the horse moved up closer in the open window of the trailer.

The horse looked right back at him and jerked on the tie rope with a definite attitude.

"Great mover, too," Jackson said. "A complete waste of talent."

"Nobody can stay on him, you say?"

"Nope. They get scared and step off. He's bad to rear."

Monte looked at the horse some more.

Cactus looked at him rebelliously.

"Not exactly what you'd call a soft eye," Monte said.

Clint and Jackson laughed.

Monte thought about it.

Cactus thought about it.

"Let me get on him," Monte said.

"Mon-te!"

His mother's voice made him turn to see the five women still standing on the porch, all of them watching and listening.

"You are not well yet," Bobbie Ann said firmly. "Do not go near that horse. Do you want to be back in the hospital again?"

"I won't be," he said. "I just want to see if I can stay on him."

He turned back to the horse.

"You have lost your mind!" LydaAnn shouted. "If you get hurt again right now, Mon, you may never ride anything else. Not even a dead-broke, retired show horse."

Of course, Delia had to join in the chorus.

"Don't get on him, Monte," she said. "It's not worth the risk."

But risk was what he lived for.

And this was his chance to prove himself to his brothers.

"Get him out," he said to Clint.

Clint started for the back of the trailer, then hesitated.

"You sure?" he said.

"Monte, please don't do this," Bobbie Ann called.

Her voice was shaking because she was scared. Monte had never realized before how scared she must've been to know he was getting on bull after bull. Actually, he had barely even thought about it.

He turned to smile at her.

"Don't worry, Ma," he said. "This horse doesn't look near as tough as any bull I ever got on."

Already the excitement was starting to rise in his blood.

"Looks are deceiving," she said. "And besides rearing, he bites and kicks, too."

But Monte turned back to his brothers.

"I want to get on him," he said.

Jackson opened the trailer door and Clint went in to untie the prickly horse called Cactus.

Monte's heart began to beat faster. He hadn't realized until now how much he'd been wanting a good, wild ride.

If he could make it.

All he had to do was ignore the pain in his back and the sudden, brand-new fear that was melting his bones.

It didn't matter to Monte that the whole gaggle of females had followed the men and the horse up to his barn or that Jo Lena had seen their ragged parade and had come to join them. The fear had shot him right through any dread of embarrassment and out the other side. All he wanted was to conquer this unaccustomed terror.

He had to get past the shock of this feeling before he could even deal with what to do. The entire distance from the trailer to the barn and inside to the crossties, he had suffered through the pictures flashing across

184

his mind, over and sideways, up and down, moments from that last ride on Old Brindle.

This fear had been born deep inside him that night, he realized. The fear of never riding again was mixed with the fear of finally getting killed in one of the hundreds of dangerous spots he'd put himself in, and that was what had been resting like a rock inside him. That was the main thing that had made him come home and then to hunt solitude.

Because when he'd lain flat on his back in the dust, he'd been afraid he was crippled for life. Never once had he considered that it might be his mental toughness that was crippled instead of his body.

Ruthlessly, he forced his thoughts to the positive. He wasn't a complete stranger to fear. Anybody who got on a bull or a bronc was afraid, but always, in Monte's case, the excitement and the anticipation of the thrill and the challenge had been much stronger than any dread. Now his fright was stronger, but all that meant was that he had to be stronger to fight it and soon the thrill would come back.

It had to. His very survival was at stake. Every ounce of his self-respect — what little he had left — was on the line.

As he and Clint clipped the crossties to

the halter, Monte took deep breaths of the hay-and-horse scented air and, in the primal way of one animal learning about another, he began to immerse himself in the horse instead of wanting to get away from him. He watched his way of accepting the restraints — his eye, his stance, his tension. When the fear swelled inside Monte again, he held it back by starting to visualize this ride. He concentrated on that.

He called on all his instincts to take over and blot out the fear.

"Want me to saddle him?"

It took a second for Monte to realize that Clint was talking to him. Another second, and he heard the tone of voice. Clint had sensed his fright.

If Clint had sensed it, the horse most certainly had done so, too. He started to take deep, calming breaths.

"No, thanks. I'll do it."

Monte went to the saddle rack for his old work saddle.

"Watch him," Jackson said from behind Monte. "He tries to bite and kick during saddling. He nearly got me twice."

"Now let's see," Clint said lightly. "That was just before you stepped up on him and then stepped right off again, right?"

"At least I had a bum leg for an excuse,"

Jackson said in the same careless tone, "and enough sense to know that if he started over backward, I couldn't get off him quick enough."

"Mmm-hmm," Clint said thoughtfully.

Jackson waited a beat.

"What was *your* excuse, Clint?" he said.

Clint considered.

"Sheer terror," he said.

They all laughed, but as Monte turned with the saddle in his arms and started toward the horse, both his brothers looked at him seriously.

"He's *bad* to bite," Jackson said.

"As you mount, he'll kick at your leg that's still on the ground," Clint said.

"Thanks for the warnings," Monte said.

His heart was beating triple time, yet the deep breathing was helping and his steely determination was rising. He had no choice — he had to at least get on this horse or he could never look himself in the eye again. It'd be no disgrace if he couldn't ride him but it certainly would be if he couldn't try him.

It was just that simple.

He focused his thoughts as he reached the horse and eased the saddle and pad onto his back.

"Longeing him only gets him warmed up

and excited," Jackson said. "He could go at a long trot from here to Oklahoma and never tire out."

So far, so good. The horse was standing quiet.

Then he danced a little and pulled his head around enough to see Monte. Monte watched him from the corner of his eye while he stepped in close and fastened the cinch.

Then he let Clint help him get the bit in his mouth and the bridle on.

"Outside," Monte said in a voice that came out far more relaxed and confident than he'd ever expected.

His heart was still beating fast but it was calming. He unsnapped the halter and let it hang. Then he took Cactus by the reins and started leading him down the barn aisle toward the round pen.

Clint and Jackson followed and, as Monte went in, they closed the gate and came to hold the horse's head until he could mount.

"Need a hand up?"

"No, thanks."

Monte stuck his foot in the stirrup and Cactus kicked at the leg he was standing on, fast as lightning. Monte jumped and got it into the air so the horse missed, then bounced that foot on the ground one more time before Cactus could recover. Monte landed in the saddle.

Clint and Jackson let go and stepped out of the way. They went to sit on the fence.

Monte glimpsed Bobbie Ann's face, and Jo Lena's, both wide-eyed and worried. He pushed them out of his mind. This was between him and Cactus and nobody else.

"Monte, be careful," Jo Lena called.

But Monte barely heard her. He kept his eye on the stud horse's ears and got him moving along the fence.

So far, he was riding him. So far, Cactus hadn't even offered to buck, much less rear. Monte kept him at a trot.

His old excitement began flooding through the fear in his veins.

Maybe he could ride him. That'd be a real satisfaction, even if it weren't for the fact that nobody else had been able to do it. That fact would only make a victory sweeter.

The next moment, Cactus was up in the air. It truly did seem to happen instantaneously, but it hadn't because Monte had sensed it coming. There'd been no warning, but his legs had gripped the horse tighter so he was still in the saddle while the horse stood and stretched his front legs to reach for the sky.

189

Monte waited, willing himself to keep breathing. He'd go back down in a minute. Surely he would.

Instead, Cactus took a couple of steps on his hind feet and then a couple more.

Instinct took over. Monte's back and his bones remembered what it was like to hit the ground with that terrible force and he thought about the fact that if the horse fell on him it would kill him.

Instinct told him to get off now, while he still could. Instinct said to let go and throw himself to one side.

He hung on, anyway. He'd always been fast and he could probably get out of the way in time.

That was what he chose to believe. He believed it.

Cactus walked around a little more, took several more steps. Monte stayed on.

Finally after what seemed an age and must have been at least two or three minutes, Cactus dropped to earth again and started trotting the same as before. Monte took a deep breath and felt power flow into him with the air.

He had won. No matter what happened now, he had won. Even if he got thrown now, he had won. The fear was cut in half, back to its old size. He could still ride. He hadn't lost his nerve. His body was healing and his mental toughness was back.

Cactus went peacefully halfway around the pen before he began to buck. This was nothing now. He gave it a good try, seemingly with all his heart, but Monte wasn't going off.

He might not ever go off this horse. He might not ever get bucked off a horse again. He'd probably get thrown by some bulls but that was okay because he'd at least be riding bulls again.

Finally, the bucking stopped and Cactus went peacefully around the pen four times, never offering to rear again. Monte relaxed in the saddle and used the opportunity to actually teach the horse to give his head a little.

Then, wanting to stop on a good note, he told the horse "whoa" and got off. He led him across the pen toward his brothers with Cactus walking at his side, peaceful as an old show horse.

Clint and Jackson climbed down and shook his hand, slapped him on the shoulder.

They met his eyes with a different attitude.

He wasn't the little brother anymore. They would have to deal with him now.

Monte sensed that change in them the same way Clint had felt Monte's fear.

Sometimes brothers did that, he was thinking.

Chapter Nine

There was a certain satisfaction to sitting still and doing something useful. It seemed funny that a man could live thirty-one years before he found that out, but it was true for him.

Monte stood up, stretched and shifted around to the other side of the newel post. From the cloth tool belt spread out on the stair step, he picked a thinner awl, one that would fit into the finer edges of the carvings, and went back to work taking the layers and layers of old varnish off the oak wood.

This house was going to be a showplace. When he bought the ranch he would never have imagined this house had been built with such care, but after three weeks of peeling and washing and stripping away wallpaper and grime and varnish and paint, he was really beginning to admire it.

He worked, sitting in the same position, fifteen minutes by his watch, then he put down his tool, straightened his back, arched it and rubbed the small of it with one hand.

Going up on tiptoe, he stretched again, reaching first for the banister rail above his head, next for his toes. After that, he did knee bends and lunges, counting them out, adding one to each set over the number he'd done the day before.

No matter how satisfying it might be to sit around and make something beautiful, he had to keep in shape. After all, he was laying in wait for a whole new bunch of bad, bad bulls while he experimented with the idea that time heals everything. It was fast healing his bones and muscles but it wasn't making much progress with his conscience.

He had to admit that it was healing his friendship with Jo Lena, though. At supper each night, they were falling back into their old high-school ways of telling each other all the happenings of their days. Why, since she had resumed her evening rides on the Rocking M, she even talked to him about her visits to the chapel and how much strength they gave her.

No matter what anybody said, that was a personal subject. And she trusted him with it.

Maybe they would end up being true friends again, even if they couldn't be anything more.

They couldn't. Because Jo Lena didn't know

what had really happened to Scotty.

His mind sheared away from his traitorous little voice of truth and he turned toward the stairs to get back to work.

There was also a downside to sitting still and doing something useful: it gave a man too much time to remember.

Something thudded against the front door. It did it again and he got up, laid down his tool and started across the room.

Before he could get there, it swung open. Jo Lena came through it backward, half bent over from carrying a huge, round tray covered with pies. Monte hurried to help her with it.

"Why didn't you yell?"

"I thought you were gone," she said breathlessly. "I didn't see your truck."

"It's out back."

"I need your oven."

"Sorry," he said as she let him take half the weight of the tray, "it's in use. I'm roasting a turkey for lunch."

Her eyes widened and flew to his, believing him for that one split second. Deep blue pools, they were, deep enough for a man to drown in.

Then she made a face at him.

"Instead of cracking pitiful jokes, you'd best build yourself a spit and a fire in the yard, mister, because I'm taking that oven."

He laughed.

It pleased him, somehow, that she would come bursting into his house expecting to do as she pleased in it.

"Mouthy as you are, you're still a great relief," he said. "When the door flew open like that, I thought it was the Clean Team on another rampage."

"I wish they'd rampage into my house," she said as they balanced the tray and carried it across the living room. "It's filthy and that's driving me crazy, but I don't have time to do anything about it."

"You and Lily should come up here and sleep on my clean floor."

She rolled her eyes and blushed a little, as if he'd made a decidedly improper proposition. As if she, too, had found it as sensual as he did for them to wake up in the same room.

Jo Lena looked as appealing in that moment as he'd ever seen her, hurrying to his kitchen with her cheeks flushed pink, her face streaked with flour. Wisps of her silky hair were escaping from her one thick braid, and her eyes were shining bright with purpose.

With excitement? Was she as glad to be with him right now as he was to be with her?

Her full lips were smiling at him. She looked extremely kissable.

"I'm not coming up here to sleep on your floor," she said. "All you want is for me to make biscuits for your breakfast and I'm not about to fall for that."

It's not biscuits. I want you here to look at. I want to see your eyes all hazed with sleep when you first wake up and your mouth half smiling from that last sweet dream.

He clamped his lips together to hold back those words or any other words that might tumble out and get him in trouble. They were going through the kitchen door. He tried to take the whole weight of the tray.

"No, no," she said. "Let me balance it. I don't have time to deal with broken glass and making more pies."

"Jo Lena, have you ever heard of those throwaway tinfoil-type pie plates?"

"Pies taste better in glass," she said firmly. "They look better, too."

They got the tray to the table and set it down. Jo Lena ran to the oven and turned it on.

Monte shook his head ruefully.

"Jo Lena, Jo Lena, Jo Lena, that makes no sense — it could never be scientifically proven. You're an artist, not a business-woman, and you can't be making any profits this way. I need to manage —"

She interrupted him.

"People bring the plates *back,* Mr. Smart Money," she said sassily, stalking toward him with her hands on her hips.

He held her gaze with his.

"Typical Jo Lena," he said idly. "Trusting everyone."

"I know," she said wryly. "You'd think I'd have learned my lesson by now, wouldn't you?"

She reached the table and looked at him for a moment longer, then bent over the pies, checking to see they hadn't been damaged in transit. Quickly she went to the sink, washed her hands and came back to adjust a bit of dough on their edges here and there.

He bit his tongue. How stupid could he be?

Suddenly she looked up into his eyes.

"I trust you now, though, Monte."

His heart lurched with a combination of thrill and dismay. She couldn't. She mustn't. He couldn't let her make any false assumptions about him.

Then her mischievous smile played on her lips.

"I trust you to lend me your oven and then help me get these pies delivered. You will, won't you?"

His heart recovered but yet it warmed, too.

That was why he loved it that she had let herself in and taken over his house. She trusted him to give her the help she needed. At least, she trusted him that much. Only that much, which was perfect.

It lightened his heart. It made him want to laugh.

"Only if you'll help me scrape varnish while they cook."

"They'll take an hour. I have to get a cake out of my oven in forty-five minutes. Can I have a break in my varnish scraping long enough to do that?"

"If you hurry right back."

"Tyrant."

"I can be bribed."

She laughed. He loved that husky laugh of hers — he'd missed hearing it far more times than he wanted to admit during the last six years.

"These are due at the Gardiner family reunion in only a couple of hours," she said without looking down at the pies in question. "It takes an hour for them to bake and twenty minutes to drive to the Gardiner ranch and ten minutes or so for the oven to preheat."

They couldn't either one break the look between them. It held them captive.

"If you'd called ahead, I'd have already turned the oven on."

She widened her eyes like an indignant girl. Like the girl she used to be.

"But I didn't think you were here!"

He couldn't even move, much less look away from her.

"Try me, Jo Lena," he said. "No matter what it is you're thinking, always try me."

She waited a long heartbeat before she answered.

"No matter what?" she said softly.

"Right."

He drew in a deep, ragged breath.

Never, never in all the thirty-one years of his life had he known how much he could need to kiss a woman. Jo Lena. To kiss Jo Lena.

"Always?" she said, more softly still.

"Jo Lena . . ." he said, his voice hoarse and rough in his throat.

She was looking up at him with those October-sky eyes of hers.

Then he *was* moving, after all — leaning across the small square table to take her mouth with his.

Her mouth tasted sweet. And spicy-strong as sourwood honey.

Her lips felt so intriguing — so blessedly familiar and so startlingly new at the very same time. He could never stop kissing her until he figured out which it was.

They moved around the table, met at the corner without ever breaking the kiss, without ever knowing they would go there, without ever considering they'd stay where they were.

And then she was in his arms, like another miracle happening, and she held him around the shoulders as if she would protect him from something. Or someone. Or somewhere.

That took away his mind.

It took away his strength, his power, his will, his heart.

He had to hold on to his heart because she would never keep it. Not anymore.

But he couldn't pull away because he was kissing her and she was kissing him back, giving him heat and light and air.

Giving him life.

Finally, the oven dinged. Slowly, reluctantly, Jo Lena broke the kiss. Her blue eyes soft and filled with their kiss, she looked up and touched his cheek before she turned away.

"I've got to get these pies to baking," she said.

Monte pretended to ignore Lily Rae and

Jo Lena while they saddled Annie out in the aisle of his barn and he cleaned the stall. He scooped up a big forkful of shavings and manure and turned to toss it into the purple plastic tub. The sight of it made him grin.

He bet there was no other big, bad bull rider in the country who had purple horse equipment all over his barn.

Lil had picked it out, of course. For her new horse, Annie. It made absolutely no difference to her whether he sold Annie to Jo Lena or not. And, actually, none to him or Jo Lena. No matter what the adults said and no matter what the registration papers said, Annie was Lily Rae's horse.

The little rascal was getting pretty good at riding her, too.

"Mommy, I think Monte should come check this cinch," she was saying. "He's so strong he can pull it tighter."

Jo Lena gave a low, husky chuckle that made him want to go out there and just look at her, if nothing else. He wasn't going to let himself kiss her again. He would not. It had been a week since then and if he could get through a week without another kiss, he could keep right on doing without.

That kind of closeness had no future for him and Jo Lena.

"Any tighter and poor Annie will be

202

gasping for breath," she said. "She has to get air in her lungs if you want her to carry you around."

Monte scooped up another forkful and pitched it. He wouldn't go out there. They were perfectly capable of saddling a horse without him and, besides, it wasn't good for them to depend on him for everything.

Well, "everything" was an exaggeration. Yet the three of them were spending a lot of time together lately. Too much time, really.

He enjoyed helping them out and he needed to because they were certainly helping him. Jo Lena's cooking and Lily's entertainment had certainly contributed to his speedy healing.

But the day would come when he'd go back to riding bulls, and keeping a little distance now would help prepare them for that day. And him, too.

That was the reason he'd told Lily Rae her mama could help her saddle.

No. The real reason he was hiding in a nine-by-twelve stall all by himself was much more selfish. He was trying to keep himself away from Jo Lena. He was trying to learn to get his feelings under control and be nothing to her but a friend.

He scooped up another forkful of bedding and manure and threw it into the tub.

There. He was making great progress facing up to *some* truths, at least.

"Monte," Lily Rae called, "I'm ready now. Come on out to the round pen, okay?"

He looked around and saw her standing tiny in the open doorway of the stall, holding the reins with Annie looming huge behind her. She was perfectly at ease.

She had her head cocked to one side and her eyebrows raised, waiting for his answer. The hat she wore was a battered straw little-cowgirl model with a pink-and-white braided hatband fastened with a red plastic heart.

Monte spoke before he thought.

"We'd better get you a new hat before the rodeo parade comes up," he said. "If you're riding a big horse like Annie and not a pony, I'm thinking you need a serious hat."

He should've kept his mouth shut. He shouldn't let these two blue-eyed females depend on him when he wouldn't be around forever.

Too late. Lily Rae lit up like a candle and pumped her free arm in the air in victory.

"All *right!*" she said. "I need *at least* a thirty X Resistol. No, wait, maybe a hundred X — like LydaAnn's."

"Only felt hats are judged by their X's," Monte said, barely keeping his face straight and his tone firm. "I'm talkin' *straw* hat, here, Lil."

Lily Rae shrugged philosophically.

"Well," she said, "winter will come."

She led Annie away, clopping down the aisle toward the open barn door on their way out to the round pen. Just before they stepped outside the barn, she called back over her shoulder.

"I need a serious winter hat, too, Monte."

Jo Lena and Monte both burst out laughing.

"I'm afraid we should have a little heart-to-heart about good manners and being greedy," she said, glancing in at him as she went toward the cart with the grooming equipment. "And that's your job, Monte. You started this business of buying her whatever she wants."

She was still smiling but there was something extraserious in her tone of voice.

"Not me," he said lightly. "I'm not the one who made her a little clotheshorse to begin with."

"Well, it wasn't me, either," she said. "I haven't had the money for that."

There it was again — that brave attempt to sound cheerful and normal.

"I've gotta get out there," she said, dumping the brushes and combs and

205

starting for the door. "She's liable to fall off the fence trying to mount all by herself."

Monte threw one more forkful, then he followed her. Annie was good and steady, true, but no horse could be totally predictable all the time — and the same was true of a child.

The same was also true of adults.

Jo Lena hadn't had that miserable, worried edge to her voice for ages — not since that first day when she'd thought she'd have to move out of her house because he'd bought it. He needed to find out what was wrong now.

They were both inside the round pen already. Jo Lena was bending over to give Lily a boost up into the saddle. Lily was frowning and shaking her head.

"Monte!" she called when she saw him. "Come and see! I can mount all by myself."

Jo Lena stood straight, turned toward him and threw up her hands in a pantomime of frustration.

Monte walked toward them. At that moment, all he wanted was to make her smile.

"Okay, Lil," he called. "Mount up."

Lily Rae led Annie to the fence, told her "Whoa," climbed up onto the next-to-top rail and stepped off it. She gave herself a push-off, which was the only way she landed in the saddle because she'd left the mare a leg length away from the fence.

Grinning from ear to ear, Lily rode off around the pen while Jo Lena just walked over to the fence and leaned her head against it, covering her face with her hands.

Monte walked up to her on the outside.

"What's the matter?" he said lightly. "That didn't scare you, did it? Just wait until she clucks her into a trot and runs alongside to mount."

To his shock, when she raised her face, Jo Lena had tears in her eyes. She didn't answer, just looked at him.

He reached through the fence and touched her hair.

"What's the matter, Jo?" he said softly.

"Nothing. She just scared me, that's all."

He searched her eyes, now a dark blue and clouded with storms.

Protectiveness surged in him. He was going to find out what was wrong with her if it took him the rest of the evening.

"I was only kidding," he said lightly. "Some kids never go through that Pony Express phase."

She tried to laugh.

"Listen to you. Dr. Monte McMahan, child behavior expert."

He grinned, trying to cheer her up.

"Maybe Lil will be one of 'em," he said. "Maybe she'll just hold her mount still and do a broad jump from the fence every time."

"And maybe I won't be there to see it," Jo Lena said, her voice catching on the last word.

She straightened her shoulders as a tear ran down her cheek.

Monte wiped it away with his thumb.

"All right," he said firmly. "Tell me."

"They're actually going ahead with the custody suit. Lily's grandparents. They've told a judge she should live with them."

"Did he think they have good reasons?"

"Ten or twelve million of 'em. All dollars."

"You got a lawyer?"

She shook her head.

"I don't even know where to start."

Monte set his jaw to hold back a sharp retort. He had offered to nip this problem in the bud and she'd turned him down flat.

"I don't have any money. . . ."

She caught herself, bit back the rest of the sentence and turned away to set her eyes on Lily. Leaning back against the fence, she crossed her arms in front of her as if to tell him to leave her alone.

Monte stood beside her, outside the

fence. He propped one foot on the bottom rail, folded his arms along the top one and stared off into the near distance. Jo Lena was proud and she had refused to accept his help in this lawyer dilemma, and she had every right to do so.

After all, hadn't he just been telling himself that it wasn't good for her and Lily to depend on him too much?

He turned back and looked at Lily Rae. Annie was jogging around the pen like an old show horse with Lily sitting proudly in the saddle.

"You're doing great, Lil," he called. "Just remember — heels down, back straight."

She turned and flashed him a huge smile.

"Thanks, Monte," she called back. "I won't forget."

The smile she gave him warmed him nearly as much as the trusting tone of her voice. She did depend on him — as proved by her confidence in informing him that she'd be needing a serious winter hat.

Just remembering that made him grin. She did adore him, as LydaAnn was always pointing out.

And he was pretty crazy about her, truth be known.

She couldn't go live with her grandparents. That would tear up her whole life and break her spirit, not to mention Jo Lena's heart.

Maybe he'd make a couple of calls, see what he could do.

The main reason he went over to the Rocking M with Jo Lena and Lily Rae for supper that Friday night was the water-melon-seed-spitting contest. Lily Rae had challenged him to a duel, and he knew he'd never hear the end of it if he chickened out.

If it hadn't been for that, he'd have stayed home to tear out the flimsy wall that made a pantry of one corner of the kitchen. For a historical restoration, the dimensions of the rooms needed to be back to their original floor plan.

But, after a while, it seemed, there was a limit to the satisfaction he could take from staying in one place and doing something useful. Evidently, there was also a limit to his need for solitude, because he didn't mind being in the middle of his entire family, fending off their questions and com-ments, and missing John and his dad every once in a while when he glanced around the circle of faces that surrounded him.

Of course, with Dad it was a good sort of miss when he remembered how he'd ham-mered at Monte sometimes about his wild behavior and the fact he never wanted to "stay hitched" to the mundane chores of the ranch. Dad had been proud of him, too, though. He'd bragged about the daring rides Monte made and the skill and nerve it took to make them.

At the end, though, Dad hadn't had a good word to say about him.

Monte shook his head to keep away all the old, bad memories from creeping up on him and got up from his chair. Conversation was lagging now and the adults were doing nothing but watching Lily Rae and Maegan trying to learn to turn somersaults on the grass.

He turned to Jo Lena.

"Want some company on your evening ride?" he said.

Startled, she looked up at him.

"Sure."

She turned to Bobbie Ann.

"Can you watch Lily . . . ?"

Bobbie Ann was already waving them away.

"Don't even think about it," she said.

So he and Jo Lena walked quietly toward the barn, side by side. The ranch spread out around them, everything in order, the animals and people all in their places — settling into contentment after being fed.

"Scooter loves these rides," Jo Lena said. "There's just something about twilight."

"That's 'cause he's already had his supper," he said. "Try taking him out before and see how much he loves it."

They laughed and joked like that while they got the horses out, saddled them and rode off. Under the live oaks along the river behind the barn and Manuel's house, then up the sloping hills to the west, until they reached a ridge where they had a view for miles.

"See how the sunlight hits the cross on the chapel?" Jo Lena said.

It was beautiful.

"Makes it look lit from inside," Monte said.

"Did you know you can see the chapel from Jackson and Darcy's new house and Cait and Clint's, too?" she said.

He shook his head. He didn't know that and he didn't want to visit the chapel right now. God had been what he and Dad had fought about and God had deserted him ever since.

"How about we go up on the bluff by the waterfall?" he said.

Jo Lena turned quickly to look at him and he realized what he'd done. Unwittingly, without thinking, he'd suggested one of their old haunts.

What was the matter with him? Was he losing his mind or what?

"If you want to," he said quickly.

"You know, Monte," she said. "I really don't. Let's just ride along the ridges and go back by the road before dark."

"Sure," he said.

He felt a quick, unreasonable stab of disappointment.

She didn't want to be out with him after dark. She'd been behaving a little differently, come to think of it, ever since that kiss in the kitchen. Maybe it had shaken her just as much as it had him. Maybe she'd made the same resolve he had, which was not to get too close, to keep this just a friendship.

Which was exactly what he'd vowed to do, too, wasn't it?

Or she might not even be thinking that much about him.

He looked straight ahead and rode along the ridge until they came to a different bend of the river from where he'd meant to go, but a view that would take a man's breath, nevertheless. This time of year, the river ran green as emerald and clear, and this time of day, the sun glinted off it in a golden glow.

From far off in the brush, some quail called. Overhead, against the blue sky, a hawk swooped and swayed and rode the wind.

It was a long way from here to any border of the ranch. Within it, all was quiet right now, and all was well.

Words came out of him, unbidden. Unknown to him.

"I love this place," he said. "The Rocking M. No place else will ever really be home."

Chapter Ten

Monte lost that peaceful moment, though, almost before it had passed.

"Why, Monte, you sound like a whole new man," Jo Lena said. "I never thought I'd hear you say that."

She sounded so pleased that it scared him.

"Neither did I," he said. "I don't know what I was thinking."

They laughed but he wasn't joking. Jo Lena had certainly changed since that first day he'd come back home and she'd been wanting his horse but not him. And the first day he went to her house and she'd tried to run him off.

Now she was happy he might stay. Well, *he* hadn't changed from the man he'd been then or the man he'd been six years ago, and if she really knew him, she'd be singing a different tune. No way was he a whole new man.

He turned his horse and led the way down off the low bluff.

He didn't even understand why he'd suggested this little trail ride for two. He had no clue what it was about Jo Lena that kept drawing him into situations where he knew he'd better not be.

That kiss had been the prime example of that. It had made him want more of her kisses and it had made him feel more protective of her. And, probably, it had made her depend on him, too.

Which would never do. He hadn't let anyone depend on him for six years and he wasn't going to start now. He wasn't going to depend on anyone, either, not even for sweet, sweet kisses. Those were the reasons he should avoid being alone with her.

But he'd kept on coming around her, going down to her house on any excuse, and he'd let himself be included in this little get-together tonight and then he'd gotten her off to herself again. He was going to have to start listening to his head, that was for sure.

What was it about her that kept drawing him to her?

He'd been pretty peaceful there for a while, before he had kissed her.

For several days now, he'd thought the trouble was physical desire but that wasn't the heart of it. The maddening thing was that he had no clue what was.

They reached the bottom of the bluff and trotted onto the road.

"Scooter wants to stretch his legs a little," Jo Lena said.

"Then let's do it," he said.

They loped all the way back to the barn without talking.

After they'd put up the horses and gone back to the house, Jo Lena immediately drifted away from him. He didn't know why, but that made him feel deserted.

"I'll get Lily and her toys rounded up," she said. "It's time to get her home and into bed."

That suited him just fine. He'd drop them off and then go knock out a wall or pick up rocks in the yard — anything that'd wear him out so he could sleep. These last few nights sleep hadn't come easy.

In fact, he was nearly as restless as he'd sometimes been on the road. He must be healing. Maybe he was well enough to ride again.

But that thought didn't hold quite the excitement it used to carry. He grinned wryly to himself: maybe he was getting addicted to stripping varnish.

He tried to stop thinking and went to help Clint and Jackson, who were putting everything back to normal before they, too, left for the night. Each of them carried one of the big rocking chairs to its usual place on the back porch.

Bobbie Ann was there, directing everything to be arranged exactly the way she wanted. When Clint and Jackson turned to go back into the yard, she caught Monte's arm.

"Sweetie, how're you doing on your house? Need any help?"

He smiled at her.

"You volunteering?"

Bobbie Ann smiled back.

"You know I've always loved to paint," she said. "And talk. We've always had fun together."

Monte patted her arm.

"We have, Ma. Sure, come on over. We'll trade tall tales and paint up a storm."

"It's a deal," she said.

He could tell she was inordinately pleased. She was practically beaming. He kicked himself mentally for not asking her to come help him before now — he knew she loved making a house beautiful by scraping and painting and papering, and that she had missed him hugely these past few years.

It was true. When he was growing up, they'd been special buddies.

"Now, remember, sugar, I'd love to hear all your tall tales, but then again, there are bound to be some things that I'm not sure I want to know. Don't forget to use your mom censor."

"I won't," he said, grinning at her.

She grinned back.

"Then we have a deal. And I'll call you ahead of time."

"Okay. I'll be looking forward to it."

The expression that lit up her face warmed him through and through.

"It'll be so much fun," she said.

She threw her arms around him in an exuberant hug, then she stood back and looked at him.

"I'll be looking forward to it, too, Monte. You'll never know how much I've missed you."

This was getting to be a bigger responsibility than he'd thought. Here was somebody else expecting him to stay.

Somebody else who didn't know everything about him. Even if she did, she would love him anyway because she was his mother. He knew that, but then again, he didn't see how she could. She would certainly be disappointed in him.

Monte smiled down at her and hugged her in return. He felt like an impostor.

When they were halfway home, Monte decided that his talk with Jo Lena about Ned could wait until morning. But then he'd definitely better tell her what he'd done and talk her into accepting it. Otherwise she might just refuse Ned outright.

He wished now he'd never made the offer to get her an attorney. Jo Lena would probably remember that and connect it with this call out of the blue from a lawyer she'd never met.

She'd suspect Ned really wasn't doing research for a book about custody cases involving grandparents versus younger relatives and furnishing pro bono counsel when needed. No, Monte needed to come clean and get her mind prepared before Ned got around to calling her.

That hadn't happened yet, or she'd have already said something about it, and it probably wouldn't be tonight. He glanced at his watch. Ten o'clock. Too late for business on the phone, surely, even for a busy, high-powered attorney like Ned.

Tomorrow morning would be fine.

He opened his mouth and surprised himself again.

"Can you go with me into San Antonio first thing in the morning, Jo?"

"Oh, I wish I could. But I can't. I've got too many orders."

He bit his lip. There he went, trying to be alone with her again. What was the matter with him?

"*I* can," Lily Rae said.

He and Jo Lena jerked their heads around to look over their shoulders. There the child sat, strapped into the back seat of Monte's pickup, happily sweaty and dirty from her romp in the yard, and so sleepy that her long eyelashes were brushing her cheeks at regular intervals.

"Sorry, pumpkin," Jo Lena said, "tomorrow's when Lupe's taking you and Maria to Taylor's birthday party, remember?"

Lily Rae forced her eyes open and mustered a pout.

"I'd rather go with Monte."

"Remember, Lil," he said, "there's a five-dollar fine for whining."

"I'm *not* whining," she whined.

"The party's at the ice-cream parlor in Fredericksburg," Jo Lena said. "And Taylor's mom told me she found some really neat favors to give all the guests."

"You know," Monte said, "that sounds like a party and a half. Too bad I wasn't invited."

"No boys allowed," Lily Rae said. "Not even big brothers."

Her head dropped back against the seat and she fell asleep.

"Thank goodness," Jo Lena said. "I'm way past dealing with a begging fit tonight."

"Me, too," Monte said. "So don't be begging me to take you to a movie before I take you home."

"No fear of that," she said. "I'm beat. A turn around the ranch on Scooter after making four dozen miniature bundt cakes and a cheesecake is a full day for anybody."

"At least you don't have to be afraid he'll bolt right out from under you like that goofy bay horse I was on."

"No. I just have to be afraid he'll get started loping and never stop, trying to prove he's just as young as he used to be."

They laughed quietly, as quietly as they'd been speaking, so as not to wake Lily Rae, and the cab of the truck wrapped around them like a private place, a safe shelter for the two of them. Outside, in the night, the moon raced in and out of the clouds. The wind was coming up.

For a mile or so, they listened to it above the growl of the diesel engine and the low, sweet music on the radio. Then they turned onto their ranch.

His ranch.

Jo Lena's ranch.

The ranch he was going to sell to Jo Lena.

They chugged along the winding road and started climbing the long hill to the two houses.

Then Jo Lena said, "I wish I didn't have too much work, to go with you tomorrow, Monte. What are you going to do in San Antonio?"

"Thought we might look at some of the stuff at the museum," he said with a careless shrug. "Start getting some ideas about furniture."

She gasped and put her hand over her heart.

"That would be such a *thrill!* I'd love to, Monte," she said. "Oh, I'm so mad that I can't go."

She gave a huge sigh and slammed her fists onto her knees.

"That's the rotten thing about having my own business. I can't get away and I can't control it. It controls me."

"You have the best job in the world," he said. "And you have complete control over whether tomorrow is a good baking day or a bad baking day."

He kept his eyes on the road but he could feel hers on his face.

"You've never known what it is to be tied down," she said.

"We'll go another day," he said. "That's all. You've invested too much to throw up your pans and run out on tomorrow's customers now."

Her obvious pleasure at his impromptu idea was making him feel downright warm inside. Was she really that disappointed about missing an outing with him?

No, McMahan. She's that disappointed about missing out on the decorating of the bed-and-breakfast, you simpleton. That's where her heart is.

"I just keep getting flashes of pictures in my head about what the house will look like when it's done," she said. "I can't wait. I can't believe you're already thinking that far ahead, Monte."

"I certainly am," he said primly. "I've already started sewing curtains for the parlor."

She slapped his arm lightly.

"I'm tired," she said, "but not tired enough to believe *that.*"

Monte slowed the truck as they reached her house, then pulled it over and parked in the turnout in front of her gate.

"Let me get Miss Birthday Party for you," he said. "She's getting pretty heavy for you to be carrying around."

"I just can't believe she's growing so

fast," Jo Lena said.

Monte heard the underlying worry in her voice again.

"Oh, Monte, I just can't bear to think . . ."

As he stepped out of the truck, he bent over and looked in at her again.

"Don't worry," he said, and held her gaze a minute. "Lily Rae is yours and that's not gonna change. Trust me."

He opened the back door and unbuckled Lily Rae's belt, gathered her up in his arms. She smiled in her sleep and snuggled her head against his chest.

His heart lurched. How could she have gotten under his skin so completely in such a short time? He'd do anything for this child.

And Jo Lena loved her a thousand times more than he did. He ought to set her mind at ease tonight, get all the worries and troubles out of her head. Then tomorrow she could enjoy her work, at least.

"I'm not even going to try to bathe her," Jo Lena whispered, going ahead up the walk to open the door. "I'll do it early in the morning."

Lily didn't stir at all when Monte laid her carefully on her bed. Jo Lena took one sandal off and he undid the other. She ran to the bathroom, wet a washcloth and came back to wash Lily's feet.

Then they left the little girl smiling in her dreams.

Monte stopped at the door to the hallway to let Jo Lena go through first. She looked up at him and brushed his arm as she slipped past him.

For one heartstopping minute he longed to lay his hand on her shoulder, turn her around and kiss her again. He wanted to, in the worst way. But he stood there with his hands at his sides.

He followed her across the living room.

"Come on in here, Monte," she said. "I bought a magazine about nineteenth-century restorations that has a lot of great pictures you should see."

She threw him a smile over her shoulder. "Want some coffee?"

No. I don't need to be sitting around the kitchen alone with you, drinking coffee and looking at magazines. It's too tempting.

But he had to talk to her and now was the time.

"If you'll give me something sweet to go with it," he said.

Like a kiss.

He bit his tongue against the words.

"I know," she said.

She turned, walking backward, and

grinned at him, mimicking what he'd said on that first day he'd ever come into this kitchen and found her with a business of her own.

"You know I jist cain't hardly drank coffee 'thout somethin' sweet to go with it, ma'am. I'd thank ye kindly fer one o' them cinnanmum muffins you got there."

"That's a whole lot exaggerated," he said, pretending his dignity was hurt. "Besides, you were so unhappy to see me and trying so hard to throw me right off this ranch, that I had to beg."

She raised her eyebrows and made a face at him. Then she went to the iron baker's rack that held a stack of magazines as she took her cell phone from her belt.

"Let me just check my messages," she said. "Cassie Moreland is supposed to leave me a final number on tomorrow's order."

She punched in the code, put the phone to her ear and listened. Her eyes grew wide and a much darker blue. They found his and grew darker still.

When she was done, she turned it off and held it in her hand.

Tears stood on her lashes.

"That was an attorney from Houston, a Mr. Ned Creighton," she said. "He's heard I might be in need of some legal services."

Monte couldn't tell whether she was relieved or upset or angry.

"He's your friend who owes you the favor, isn't he?"

"Yes."

"Is Ned good enough to save Lily Rae for me?"

"Yes."

Slowly, with her eyes still searching his, she walked across the kitchen and stood in front of him.

"I told you not to do that, Monte."

"I wouldn't have, but Ned's the only attorney I know."

She didn't even smile at that feeble attempt at humor.

"I don't know how to repay you."

"I'd rather you didn't."

"I have to."

"Sounds like you're talking debts, here, Jo Lena. I wish you'd want to do something for me because you *like* me, not because you *owe* me."

That did make her smile. It gave him hope.

"I'm thinking you once said you feel that very same way, Jo Lena."

Her smile trembled.

"I do," she said.

"Then let's just call this friendship," he

said, "and admit everybody needs help sometimes. Then we can let Ned get this custody deal nailed down."

"I've told you how I feel about needing to make it on my own."

"Nobody can," he said. "Not for a whole lifetime. Even powerful Ned himself has had to have a little help from time to time."

That distracted her a little from her stubborn resolve, as he had hoped it would.

"I've been wondering," she said, "since that day you mentioned him. What's the big favor he owes you?"

"It's a long story involving bulls and alcohol and a very bad fight," he said, "and the fact that marks on a man's record can keep him from taking the bar exam."

Her eyes narrowed as she thought that through.

"So you took the rap for Ned? For what he did? Monte? Did you get arrested in his place?"

"It was a long time ago," he said. "Are you mad at me for calling him to take your case?"

"I don't have any choice," she said.

She went to the refrigerator, opened the freezer and brought out a bag of coffee beans. Then she pulled the coffeemaker to her across the countertop and flipped up the lid.

"That is not the point at all," he said.

He was struggling to keep the conversation going between them, willing the right words to come to him that would make her talk to him some more.

"Then what is?"

She reached up to the cabinets, opened one and took down the grinder.

"The point is what's best for Lily Rae," he said. "No amount of pride or obligation should be allowed to stand in the way of that."

She whirled around to glare at him.

"Don't you think I *know* that? Don't you think that's why I'm letting you *do* this?"

She poured beans into the grinder and slammed it into action.

Once the noise was over, Monte took his chance.

"Don't *you* know there's no way you're alone in this, Jo?"

She was still for a minute, her head down. Finally, she filled the pot with water, poured it into the machine, dumped in the coffee and flicked it on. All without speaking.

Then she turned and looked at him. She reached back and braced herself on the edge of the counter.

"It's a feeling like falling to let myself depend on you," she said. "I've trained myself so hard for so long to depend on God and me and no one else."

Her eyes went bright with tears and she started toward him.

"But it's a wonderful feeling of relief, too," she said. "I'm grateful to God and to you, Monte, with all my heart. Thank you."

A sob caught on the last word.

He stood up, stepped away from the table and took her in his arms. Her tears warmed his skin through his shirt.

"Monte," she said, "I love you. I've never stopped loving you."

His heart quit beating. Surely he hadn't heard her right. What would he do? She couldn't love him. He couldn't let her love him.

"Don't, Jo," he mumbled. "Don't love me."

She pulled back and looked up at him, started wiping her tears with her sleeve.

"I don't have a choice about that, either," she said. "I've always loved you, ever since I can remember."

She walked past him and sat down at the table.

"God gave you to me to love," she said.

"Don't worry. You don't have to love me back."

Anger slashed through his fear.

"You don't even have a clue what you're talking about, Jo Lena. Because you don't have a clue about who and what I am."

She hunched her shoulder and wiped her face one last time. Then she sat up straight and eyed him up and down.

"I know more about who you are than your mother does," she said.

He turned and started pacing, the blood rising in him so fast from all the memories and regrets, that he couldn't stand still.

There was no hope for it. He'd have to tell her. He had to stop this madness right now.

"You are such an innocent, Jo Lena. I cannot believe you still feel this way after what I did to you."

"You left me without a word of goodbye when I needed you more than I ever needed anyone in my whole life," she said. "But I've forgiven you for that."

"That's not even the half of it."

He had to get out of this now or he'd never be able to. He'd have to be brutal, but in the long run it'd be best for her. She would thank him for it someday.

"Oh?"

She crossed her arms over her chest.

"Then what *is* the half of it, Monte?"

He made the turn to pace back toward her and saw that she was looking at him steadily, her eyes wet but not crying, waiting. Just waiting for him to confess his most heinous sin.

"I killed Scotty as sure as if I'd picked up a gun and shot him."

"Scotty was gored to death by a bull. I saw it with my own eyes."

"Scotty would never have been in the pen with that bull if I hadn't egged him on. I talked him into entering."

She shook her head.

"Scotty had a mind of his own," she said. "And a will of his own."

Monte felt the breath leave him. Probably, if he said the words, he'd never draw air into his lungs again. It would kill him just as he'd killed Scotty.

Fair enough. If he could shock Jo Lena back into her right mind, it'd be worth it.

He made himself stand still and look her in the eye.

"I traded bulls with him, Jo. After we drew our rides, I couldn't rest until he traded with me."

To his shock, she didn't turn a hair.

"Because you knew Sidewinder was out

233

to gore his rider and you didn't want it to be you?"

"No. Because I *thought* I knew El Paso was the toughest ride and I wanted the chance at more points."

She just sat there and stared at him.

"I've known that the whole time," she said.

Again, he thought his ears had betrayed him.

"You couldn't have."

"I was there that night, remember? Scotty came out behind the chutes and talked to me."

Monte tried to wrap his mind around that.

His mouth went so dry, he couldn't speak.

This knocked him out. If she'd known all along and she still loved him . . .

"How?" he croaked. "How can you love me?"

"None of that was your fault," she said. "Scotty was as much of a grown man as you were and he had to make his own decisions. What nearly killed me was how you deserted me without a word."

"That was unforgivable," he agreed quickly.

Surely that would help her realize that she

didn't love him. She couldn't. She just thought she did.

"I forgave you," she said. "God forgave you."

This wasn't right. It made no sense.

"God is what Dad and I fought about," he said. "God is who let the life bleed out of Scotty right there in the dirt with me on my knees over him, praying and begging for his life. Don't talk to me about God."

"God has forgiven you long ago for all of it, for everything — for deserting me, for deserting Him — for everything," she said. "He will let you know that if you'll ask Him."

"God doesn't want to hear from me," he said. "Or about me, either. Don't you be wasting your breath praying for me."

He strode past her into the living room and on out of the house as fast as he could walk without breaking into a run. His feet felt like lead on the way to the truck but he didn't turn back.

She had followed him. He knew it because she closed the door behind him. He heard the soft click beneath the low cry of the wind.

Monte threw himself into his truck, shifted into gear and drove on up the hill. He was proud as could be of the way he resisted temptation.

And he was hitting the steering wheel with fury at the risk-ducking coward he had become.

Chapter Eleven

Monte drove on up to his house because he couldn't think where else to go. He didn't want to be there, he didn't want to be anywhere, but most of all, he didn't want to be anywhere near Jo Lena with her love for him.

That was an obligation right there. If you loved somebody, you depended on them in some way, if for nothing else than to be the person you thought they were. The person you loved.

And Jo Lena didn't know him, really . . .

Yes, she does, buddy. Yes, she does. And she still says she loves you.

It was entirely too much to deal with. And yet, after all that, one part of him had wanted to turn around and go right back into her house.

That Jo Lena had a power over him. He would never forget, if he lived to be a hundred, how he'd felt when she'd put her arms around him for that kiss the other day.

Why, with that kind of power over him, she could even lead him back to God.

He slammed that thought away from him as he slammed the truck door behind him. Nobody was going to have power over him. Nobody. It was about time he got control of his own life again and stopped letting it be all connected and intertwined with other people's lives.

If he stayed around here, eventually Jo Lena would quit loving him. No matter how much she forgave the past, he was bound to disappoint her in the future so she'd change her mind about him sooner or later.

Honestly, she might be a grown woman, but she was as innocent as Lily Rae when it came to him. That was why both of them loved him — they were total innocents in a big, bad world.

He made it as far as his kitchen and was standing in the middle of it like a goose with no sense of direction when he heard the low rumble of a vehicle out on the road. Their road. Jo Lena? Who else could it be at this time of night?

What if she were coming up here to talk to him?

He turned and strode back across the dark living room. Coming in, he hadn't bothered to turn on any lights.

Deep down, he hoped he was wrong and there was nobody out there.

Talking to somebody — *anybody* — was the last thing he wanted right now, and that included Jo Lena.

But maybe something was wrong. Maybe she needed help. . . .

He cut off the thought. That was a perfect example of the situation he was in. He didn't want anybody depending on him. Not on any long-term basis. He wouldn't have it.

For something temporary, yes. He had rather enjoyed helping Jo and Lily Rae and doing what little he'd done for them, but he didn't want that from now on. He had to get out of this now or he never would.

She *loved* him? He couldn't believe it. She was out of her mind.

He reached the front window and looked out.

A pickup sat in front of Jo Lena's gate with the passenger door standing open. Some guy came running down her walk toward it and, as Monte watched, he vaulted over the gate, got in the truck, closed the door and it came roaring on up the hill toward him.

It looked vaguely familiar in the moonlight.

Then it was there, swinging into his yard, and he saw that it was Andy's battered

Ford. His old road buddies had found him.

Well. Talk about timing. If he didn't know better, he'd think God sent them.

Not that he wanted to see anybody right now, but these rowdies'd be a sure cure for sitting around here thinking about Jo Lena for the rest of the night. Distraction. That's what he needed.

"Hey, Monte!"

All four doors of the truck opened. Four guys fell out and started for the door.

Monte stepped out onto the porch.

"I'm gonna have to put up a gate down there at the highway," he said. "The way it is now, anybody can get in here."

"Better not do that unless you give your good-looking blond neighbor a key," Duffy said. "Boys, I tell you now, that's a beautiful woman. After I saw her I didn't care if we found you or not, Monte my man."

A sharp jab of jealousy stung Monte.

"Careful with your mouth, Duf," he said. "She's a friend of mine."

It wasn't that he considered Jo Lena belonged to him. He already knew he didn't want her to love him — hadn't he just been worrying about that?

But still, Duffy had no business talking about her. Or *to* her, for that matter.

"Friend of yours is fine with me," Duffy

said. "Want me to run back down there and borrow a cup of sugar?"

"Give it a rest," Monte said. "What are y'all doing out here terrorizing the countryside in the middle of the night?"

"Hunting for you," Andy said.

They all gathered around the steps, stretching and kicking the kinks out of their legs while Monte exchanged greetings with Shawn and Tater.

"So," Monte said, "want to come in for some coffee?"

"No time to brew some," Andy said. "We'll get it on the fly at the QuikTrip store."

Monte shook his head.

"Y'all in a big hurry?"

The old, hot challenge was stirring, beginning to build in his blood. They hadn't come to crash for the night or to sit around and trade lies. They'd come for him.

"Yep," Shawn said, "on our way to the big Bullnanza down in El Paso."

"Bret's asleep in the truck," Tater said, "and we're sick of being all crowded up in that back seat. Reckon you could come along and drive another vehicle?"

Nobody said anything for a couple of heartbeats.

"We hadn't heard," Andy said, "but we

thought you might be about healed up by now."

It was a delicate subject to bring up, since the rumor Monte could never ride again had been noised far and wide. All four of them looked at him and waited.

The turmoil in Monte's gut came surging together into one headlong rush of excitement.

"I'll get my gear bag," he said.

Jo Lena was trying to make herself get ready for bed when she heard the truck coming back down the road. She tried, for maybe one tenth of one second, not to go to the window — it was too dark, anyhow, to tell if Monte was with them — but her heart pulled her across the room to a spot where she could see.

When they passed her house, headed for the highway, she was leaning her forehead against the window glass and praying for strength. Those bull riders came blasting past like they were on the interstate highway and, sure enough, right behind them raced Monte's truck, with Monte driving. Dark night or not, she knew him.

The set of his head and the way he held his shoulders were unmistakable. One of his buddies was with him.

Before she could really take it in, they were gone. She stood there, anyway, crushing the curtain in her hand, watching their dust hang in the moonlight until every fleck of it had fallen back to earth.

Finally, slowly, she let go and walked through the house and into the kitchen where the light was still on.

"Dear Lord," she said. "Give me strength."

She collapsed into the chair where she'd sat when she'd told Monte he didn't have to love her back.

Well, he didn't. He didn't have to, and he didn't.

Her arms sagged heavily in her lap. She couldn't even raise them to rest on the table.

If only, *if only* she had kept her mouth shut. If only she'd never said those fateful words, *I love you.* He'd been home for weeks now and she'd loved him all that time and she'd not blurted out her feelings right to his face.

She had been proud of herself for staying so cool and balanced, she had been grateful to God for helping her know that she could make it through life just fine without Monte as her partner.

Truly she had believed they could be friends and no more.

And then she'd gone and ruined it all by telling him she loved him!

No man wanted to be blindsided like that when he hadn't declared his own feelings — especially not a man like Monte.

But she simply could not help herself. He'd already made her heart turn over when he'd been so thoughtful and sweet to carry Lily Rae in and take off her shoes. He really did love that child, whether he knew it or not.

And then, when she'd heard that message from Ned and realized Monte was going to save her baby for her when she couldn't do it for herself, she had broken apart inside and she'd wanted to hold him and kiss him and tell him over and over again that she loved him.

Well, once had been plenty. Once had done the trick. Fifteen minutes later, and he was gone.

Of course, he might be coming back. They might be going out for coffee or for a late sandwich at Hugo's, just visiting before the other guys went on down the road and Monte came home.

Of course, the last time he'd left, he'd stayed gone for six years.

He was going to keep this up and break her heart once and for all, into so many pieces she could never put it back together.

Lord, please give me strength. Dear Lord. What am I going to tell Lily Rae? Oh! And Bobbie Ann? Poor Bobbie Ann.

If only she'd kept her love for him hidden!

She would never forget how he'd gone so still when she said it. She'd felt him wanting to pull back, wanting to break the embrace.

She could still hear him mumbling, "Don't, Jo. Don't love me."

That destroyed her all over again. That was sadder than the fact he didn't love her in return.

Monte did not believe that he could be loved, he did not believe he was lovable, and that was the worst thing of all. If he couldn't believe that, he'd never be able to forgive himself.

A loud chiming song rang out. She jumped.

For a second she couldn't think what it was. Then she realized it was her cell phone.

She lifted her head. Where had she left it? On the counter by the coffeepot.

She took a long, deep shuddering breath of the delicious coffee aroma. Monte hadn't even waited for a cup of coffee, she'd scared him so bad.

A wry smile curved her lips. If she'd known, she could've poured him a cup to go.

The phone rang one more time, then quit. The voice mail would get it.

Long after the message had been left — if there was one — she sat staring into space. It might have been Monte, calling to say goodbye.

That'd be one small improvement over the last time he left her.

Jo Lena had no idea how much longer she sat there. Finally she got up and went to the counter, picked up the phone and punched in her code.

"Jo Lena?" Monte said into her ear, his voice filled with a suppressed excitement. "Would you please feed Annie and turn her out in the morning? I'm gonna be on the road for a few days. I'll have Manuel call you to see if you want him to move her over to the Rocking M so you won't have to do chores all the time."

There was a short pause, as if he had to stop and think what to say next.

"Uh, uh . . . and would you tell Lil to keep on riding every day and . . . that I'll be on the lookout for her new hat?"

Another pause.

"Thanks, Jo," he said. "Thanks for everything."

She listened some more, but that was all. Jo Lena took the phone from her ear and turned it off. She laid it on the counter and walked away from it but she could still hear his voice in her ear.

I'm gonna be on the road for a few days.

What a laugh. "A few years" would be closer to the truth.

And she'd known it since the minute she opened the door and saw that bunch of bull riders. She'd known at a glance that they'd come to get Monte.

He was gone.

Monte felt dizzy as he climbed up the wall of the chute. It was excitement, he realized, as he got into position and lowered himself down onto the bull. It wasn't pain, not fear, not even the pressure from the noise of the crowd or all the eyes on him or being surrounded again by his friends and buddies with all of them knowing what it was like to climb up on a bull and ride him and waiting to see if Monte still had what it took to do it and win.

No, it was that old, exciting feeling of power that was filling him: that fiery, crackling certainty that he could ride anything with horns and hair.

That was enough thrill to make him dizzy. He hadn't known if he'd ever feel this way again.

All his pain was gone. He wouldn't feel it anymore until this ride was over.

And all his uncertainty was gone. No more feeling that he needed to do something but he didn't know what to do or how to do it.

No more being afraid he might let somebody down. He wasn't going to disappoint anybody here this afternoon.

This was all so familiar: the smells of dirt and manure and bulls and sweat, the yells from his buddies as he adjusted his seat and they got his rope on the bull and helped him get it wrapped around his hand just right.

This was what he knew how to do. This was what he *wanted* to do.

He didn't know how to live any other kind of life.

Monte took a long deep breath and checked the wrap on his hand one more time. Then he nodded to the gate man to open the gate.

"Outside," he said.

In the split second they burst out into the arena with the bull already bucking like the champion he was and Monte balanced on his back like the champion *he* was, his excitement gave way to pure joy. The sun shone and sparkled off the bull's horns, the announcer's stand, the bleachers. The sky was endless and blue, arched above the world. The dirt smelled like damp, good earth and the bull was bucking good beneath him.

Overcoming all fear and beating a bull at his own game. No way could life be better.

Jo Lena rode Scooter toward the chapel at a trot when she really wanted to urge him into a lope, into a gallop, into a flat-out run. But Scooter wasn't so young anymore and he'd already had a run this evening.

"And we both needed it, didn't we, Scooter?"

She leaned forward to pat his neck while she tried to steady her heart. It, too, kept wanting to race on ahead.

But the reason she was here was to ask God for directions on how to get through this new — and old — rough patch in her life and she already knew that He wasn't going to say to take it at a run. She couldn't run away from the fact that Monte was gone. Or that she had dared to start dreaming that he might stay.

Or that she had started praying that he would return her love someday.

Now she had to figure out how to pray for herself and for Lily Rae, because this time she had *two* broken hearts to consider.

Of course, it was a blessing that Lily was still this young. Actually, she wasn't broken-hearted, at least not yet. She was sure that Monte would be back because he'd said "a few days" and because he was going to bring her a new hat.

Jo Lena clenched her teeth as Scooter walked into the yard of the chapel.

When Monte *didn't* come back for months, when he *didn't* bring a new hat, *that* was when Lily Rae's heart would break. In her child's view, though, right now that could never happen.

Jo Lena had tried to prepare her. She had gently suggested that Lily Rae not take Monte's words too literally and not look for him anytime soon.

But Lily Rae's faith in him was unshakable. Monte would do what he said he would do and she wasn't hearing any other possibilities, no matter how hard Jo Lena tried to get them into her head.

She heaved a big sigh as she dismounted.

Lily Rae's heart would just have to break really hard when it broke because she did not have the strength to look into those big, trusting blue eyes and try to prepare the poor baby for disappointment one more time. This would be one item on her new prayer list: for God to give Lily Rae a sense, somehow, that Monte wouldn't be coming back.

Jo Lena tied Scooter to his usual tree and started for the chapel door. She would come here every evening that she possibly could. Not only to pray for herself and Lily Rae and Bobbie Ann, but for Monte.

That was the key to surviving this entire nightmare repetition of the past: praying for Monte.

The realization came to her the minute she opened the creaking double doors and walked through them into the tiny church.

She and Lily Rae would both heal someday, even if Monte never came back. But Monte would not.

If Monte couldn't at least visit home sometimes, then he didn't believe that they loved him enough to forgive him. If he couldn't believe that they loved him, he couldn't love himself.

And if he couldn't love himself, he couldn't believe God loved him. He couldn't *let* God love him.

The person she must pray for was Monte.

Monte stood in the arena with his hands in the air in victory, listening to the crowd roar, watching the sunlight glint and sparkle, feeling the slaps on the back from his buddies.

251

"Way to go, Mont," Andy said. "You haven't lost it, man."

But, as always, what Monte really wanted to hear was his score.

"Folks, that's a ninety-six point ride right there. A-aa-nd, it's a record on this particular bull. Whaddya say to a fabulous comeback for one of this world's toughest bull riders, Monte McMahan?"

The noise got louder, although that didn't seem possible. Cowboys he didn't even know began coming up to congratulate him and Monte's competitive blood started pumping. He had a chance to get back up in the standings. A good chance. They couldn't count him out yet.

Flanked by Duffy and Andy, he left the arena with the crowd still cheering. He didn't know when he'd been happier.

"It's a sign," Duffy said, beaming nearly as much as if he'd made the ride himself. "This means we get a decent meal before we hit the road. Right, Monte?"

"Good by me," Monte said.

Andy and Duffy went to round everybody else up and Monte went to the truck.

He didn't know when he'd ever been happier.

Then he thought of that moment on the bluff, looking down at the river and feeling the ranch around him with Jo Lena at his side. Before she'd told him that she loved him.

And that minute or two when he'd carried Lily Rae into the house and she'd snuggled into his chest so trustingly. Both those moments had given him a feeling like happiness.

Maybe contentment would be the word for it.

And now, both of those blue-eyed friends of his must be discontented because he was gone.

Not to mention Bobbie Ann. He had heard the disappointment in her voice when he'd called the Rocking M. He hadn't been as lucky with that call as he'd been with the one to Jo Lena when he got her voice mail.

One part of him, though, had been hoping to hear Jo Lena's husky voice, no matter what she was feeling about him right then.

He straightened up from unfastening his chaps and shook off those thoughts. Too much responsibility. He didn't *want* anybody else's happiness depending on him.

That night, two hundred miles down the road from his big win, Tater woke him from a light doze to take his turn at driving. Monte was glad.

"I'll probably get more rest at the wheel," he muttered as they changed places.

"Hey, it's mine and Duffy's lives at stake, too, you know," Tater said. "Try to stay awake."

"No problem," Monte said. "I've been trying but I can't go into a deep sleep."

And it was all Jo Lena's fault.

He put the truck in gear and pulled it back up onto the road. She should never have told him that she loved him and put that guilt on him.

But why should he feel guilty about that? He didn't ask her to love him. He didn't try to make her love him.

All he'd been doing was helping her out a little, maybe to make up for the past.

He thought about that while the big engine hummed and Tater instantly dropped off to sleep and the wheels rolled down the dark highway.

It was so hard to believe that Jo Lena had known the whole story of Scotty's death all this time, yet she loved him anyway. How could she?

It must be true, though, or she'd never have said it. Jo Lena had a lot of pride and she'd said it, knowing that he didn't feel the same way about her.

She'd said it because she was a totally

honest person. She really did love him.

His heart warmed, and then rebelled.

If you loved someone, you needed that person. He had never allowed anyone to need him, and he wasn't about to start now.

He wrenched his mind away from Jo Lena and tried to fix it on the here and now. He had marked ninety-six points today. On Sassafras, who had rarely been ridden at all.

But right now, to tell the honest truth, he didn't even care.

The best thing about his ride had been conquering the fear again. A bull was a whole different deal from a horse and, although he'd overcome most of his fear by riding Cactus, he'd had some lingering doubts. Now they were gone.

Yet the old elation, the old competition that had driven his life for so long, hadn't stepped in to take their place.

Something had changed. Winning wasn't what it used to be.

He tried not to think about that, either.

Here he was, going down the road, doing what he loved. The other two guys were asleep, Andy's truck was somewhere behind him and there wasn't another soul on the road, anywhere.

Narrow black asphalt with a white line down the middle and one on each side. The road. The road had been his home for a long, long time.

And it still was. He gave himself a little shake. He'd better know it. The road was his home.

In the front passenger seat, Tater was snoring like a chainsaw. In the back seat, Duffy lay sprawled, his stockinged feet up against the window right behind Monte. Every once in a while, he twitched and hit the back of Monte's seat with his knee. His boots on the floorboard carried the faint scent of manure.

It surely had been a lot more pleasant when it was Lily Rae sleeping silently back there and Jo Lena in the passenger seat, talking to him and smelling pleasantly of perfume. He always thought she smelled like roses.

He grinned. Yep. It'd be a whole lot more entertaining to go down the road with Jo and Lil.

And probably a whole lot more trouble. They'd have to haul a trailer along for Annie, too.

Monte gripped the wheel hard with both hands. He was losing his mind. He didn't want to think about Lily Rae or Jo Lena — especially Jo — at all.

Chapter Twelve

Jo Lena slid the three layers of cake into the oven, then she flicked on its light and stood there for the longest time, holding on to the handle and staring through the window at the liquid yellow batter pooled in the silver metal pans, waiting to rise. She was waiting, too. Foolishly.

Monte wasn't coming back and she knew that, so what could she be waiting for? She was so worn-out that sometimes she didn't even want to move.

Other times, she couldn't remember what she'd been planning to do next.

She closed her eyes and made herself take several deep breaths. Too bad she couldn't sleep right here, standing up — then maybe she could get some rest.

Finally she checked the time.

Eleven o'clock. At night.

The filling and the frosting for a Lady Baltimore cake took a while, so she'd do both of them tomorrow. In thirty minutes, when the cake was done, she would go to bed.

Ever since Monte had left, she couldn't sleep. Tired as she always was, every night it took hours for her to go to sleep, and then she had to get up with Lily before she could get rested.

It wasn't worry keeping her awake, it was loneliness. She was so lonely she could die.

Jo Lena made herself turn around and go back to the sink where she'd dumped her dirty mixing bowls. She would get all the dishes into the dishwasher and pray while she did it.

Lord, I'm praying You'll take away my worry and give me peace instead. I'm praying You'll go to Monte and knock on his heart to let You in to give him peace, too. I'm praying You'll give me peace, no matter what he does.

Peace. If she could have some peace and twelve hours of sleep, she could cope with life. She could enjoy living once again.

"Mom-mmy?"

Startled, Jo Lena turned to look over her shoulder. Lily Rae, wide-eyed, stood in the doorway dragging the frayed baby blanket that had been her comfort for years.

"Where's Monte?" she said.

Jo Lena's heart broke. It seemed like weeks since he had been gone. Soon it would be more than a few days and then it would be weeks and then months and years.

Whatever was she going to tell this child? What *could* she tell her that wouldn't destroy her faith in all men? Her daddy had died before she ever knew him and now Monte, whom she loved like a daddy, was gone, too.

"Well, sugar," Jo Lena said, "he's gone to ride some bulls again, remember? You've been asleep, so you've probably forgotten that."

"No, I didn't. And I heard him talking to you."

She came into the kitchen and looked around, checking out the breakfast table and the back-porch entry. Jo Lena rinsed her hands and reached for the towel.

"You've really had a nice dream, haven't you? That was a *good* dream but Monte's not here, sweetheart."

She went to Lily and scooped her up in her arms.

"Come on back to bed now and get your sleep. You'll want to be rested so you and Maria can have fun tomorrow."

Lily snuggled her face into the crook of Jo Lena's neck as she often did, but only for an instant. Then she straightened up to look at Jo Lena while she carried her down the hall.

"I want Monte," she said. "I *need* to talk to him."

"What about?"

"About my hat. It won't be very long until the rodeo parade."

Quick anger flared in Jo Lena. How dare he be so cruel?

"I need to talk to him, too, sweetie. But Monte's on the road, a long way from here."

Even now, she'd listen; she'd press the phone closer to her ear and let his voice send pleasure right into the core of her if he would call.

"We could try his cell phone," Lily said. "The number's there on your blackboard."

Jo Lena set her jaw and held her little girl tighter.

"It's way too late for that tonight," she said, fighting to keep her turmoil out of her voice.

She tried to fill it with bright excitement.

"I tell you what! Let's start looking around for a hat for you ourselves because Monte might not make it back for the rodeo parade."

That was the wrong thing to say, for sure. Lily Rae stiffened and stared at her in horror. In the hallway light, her big eyes glistened with tears.

"He will! Monte said he'd get me a hat to

wear in the parade, and he *will!*"

Jo Lena carried her into her room and laid her down on her bed. She tucked the blanket in, too, since Lily Rae was clutching it as hard as she could with both arms.

But Lily Rae threw off the covers and sat right up straight again.

"Monte's my big brother," she said, tears running down her cheeks. "He wouldn't tell me a *lie!*"

Jo Lena, blinking back her own hot tears, sat down on the side of the bed and wiped Lily's away with the corner of the sheet.

Help me, Lord. Give me the right words.

"You know, pumpkin," she said, swallowing hard, "sometimes people don't get to do what they say they will but it's not a lie. They mean to do it, but they just can't."

"Monte can," Lily said. "Monte can do anything."

"Monte's human," Jo Lena said. "We have to remember that."

"He's my big brother," Lily said. "Remember *that.*"

"I am," Jo Lena said. "And I'm remembering that he really did like being your big brother, too."

To her surprise, that calmed Lily.

"He does," she said. "He likes to have a

261

little sister. LydaAnn's too big to be it any-more."

She lay down peacefully and put her head on her pillow.

For a long time, Jo Lena stroked her hair back from her flushed little face.

Tell me, Lord. Please tell me what to tell her.

Finally she spoke. "Sometimes things happen," she said softly, "that people can't control. And sometimes they have feelings that they can't control. Monte likes to ride bulls, too. You know that."

"Yeah," Lily said as sleep started creeping into her voice, "but, Mommy, you know what?"

"No, darling. What?"

"He likes *me* better."

She turned over onto her side and put her thumb into her mouth. Then she talked around it.

"I'll buy him some bulls of his own," she said.

A moment later, she was fast asleep.

The big, white bull took one good jump out of the chute and headed to the left, bucking hard. Monte stayed loose up on top of his rope and got into the rhythm. Good old Ghostbuster. He was acting true to form tonight.

Monte hooked his spurs in and was more than ready when the bull flung himself in the opposite direction and started his trademark tight spin. The pull at Monte's body first threatened to send him flying into space, then it tried to take his body apart and separate him into a million pieces.

He resisted the natural urge to stiffen and pull back. He sat on top of the whirling bull, never let his weight shift to upset his center of balance, kept one hand in the air and a smile on his face. The arena and the crowd and the lights rotated crazily around him.

When the buzzer sounded, he let go and got off.

After that, he could hear the crowd but he still couldn't see anything but the bull. Ghostbuster turned and made a halfhearted feint at him that brought a scream or two from the folks in the padded seats of the fancy new arena, then he did his famous high-speed spin one more time and lumbered off like a lamb toward the open gate waiting for him.

Monte glanced up at the lighted scoreboard as he headed back toward the chutes.

Ninety-one.

A thousand people or so were cheering for him. He had ninety-one points on this ride.

The announcer shouted that Monte'd

made it look easy and gave a whole line of gab about what a comeback Monte was making and how he still had a chance of being top man for the year. Then he asked a question that Monte didn't quite catch, so Monte just threw up his hand in a wave and kept on walking. He could care less what anybody wanted to know about him.

All he wanted was out of there.

He went straight out through the stock entrance of the huge arena and across the parking lot toward his truck.

This was Omaha. He'd done the same thing in Albuquerque — made a great ride, yet he hadn't felt the old thrill.

Even in El Paso, on the first bull since he got hurt, he'd been happy but not pumped up and flying the way he'd always been before. He could see now that that was happiness for riding through the fear, and nothing more.

If he'd had any intention at all, he'd meant to sit in his truck a while and try to figure it out. Yet the minute he slammed the door behind him, he stuck the key into the ignition and fired it up.

His mind raced. What would he do without the old thrill that had kept him on the road for so long?

It had pulled him through all the years,

good and bad. So how could it be gone?

It was, though. He knew it as he left the parking lot.

He drove out to the street, turned left and kept going without even thinking of direction.

Some famous cowboy, maybe Gary Leffew, had once said, "The day I reach down inside me for a double handful of 'want to' and come up empty is the day I hang up my chaps."

Monte glanced down. He still had his chaps on but that didn't mean much. He had to admit it. His "want to" was gone.

Without knowing another thing for sure, he knew that much.

He was up for another bull tonight but somebody else would have to ride him. Right now what he had to do was be alone to think this through.

The light turned red in front of him and he stopped. Maybe he was just getting too old for the game. Maybe he wasn't scared *enough*, anymore. It was overcoming the fear and beating the bull that kept a rider going back time after time.

The green arrow showed and he turned left. Maybe when Jo Lena told him that she forgave him, it had robbed him of that old need to get the best of the bulls for Scotty's sake.

Jo Lena forgave him. She'd known all this time and she still forgave him. Could that *possibly* be true?

He blasted up the ramp to the interstate and watched the mirror until he could slip into the stream of traffic. No way was he going to think about Jo Lena.

What he had to think about was what had gone wrong with his *life*. Riding bulls was the one thing he knew he could do. Riding bulls *was* his life.

He'd made a fantastic ride this afternoon and he'd known it'd go great from the very first jump the bull had made. Any other time, that ride would've pumped him up something fierce.

Any other time, just getting *onto* a bull would've pumped him up.

Any other time, that excitement would've been blazing through him.

Instead, he'd gotten a bigger thrill out of scraping off old varnish and knocking down a wall or two. For a thirty-one-year-old man, that was a pitiful thing to admit.

The traffic was heavy and he was running in the fast lane, as always, when he noticed the billboard up ahead for Longhorn Western Wear in the Stockyards. Next Exit. He started checking the mirror for chances to move across to the outside lane as he reached for his cell phone.

Andy answered on the first ring.

"Where *are* you, man? Everybody's been looking for you."

"Something's come up. I'll see you guys later."

"You're not riding your other bull?"

"Nope."

Andy was quiet for a minute, trying to figure it out.

"Hey," he said. "What happened?"

"Nothing," Monte said. "No problem, just headin' on home."

There was another short wait before Andy realized Monte wasn't going to say anything more.

"Gotcha. Good luck, Monte."

"Same to y'all. Be careful."

"Will do."

It seemed so strange to be leaving it all behind — and not because he *couldn't* do it anymore but because he *wouldn't*.

"Come by when you can," Monte said.

"Sure thing."

Monte turned his phone off and dropped it into the console.

At least now he knew where he was going.

Jo Lena piddled around the barn, sweeping the aisle and straightening up the tack room, so Lily Rae could stay with Annie a little while longer. Ever since Monte had been gone, Lily Rae had clung to the mare.

Really, in a child that young, her faithfulness was remarkable. Jo Lena had done the chores, morning and night, every day and Lily had come to the barn with her every time.

"We're going to have so much fun, Annie," she said. "I'll ride you and Monte will ride some other horse from the Rocking M. Whoever it is, though, you'll be prettier. I promise."

Jo Lena swept the last of the dirt out the door and turned to look at them.

Lily stood on a mounting block in the middle of the aisle, pretending to braid Annie's mane. She had tried and tried to learn to braid, but it was still a little bit beyond her skills, so she twisted each section of mane and fastened it with one of the small rubber bands made for that purpose.

It took forever for her to get the band onto the hair and wrap it twice but she never gave up. So far, in the last thirty minutes, she had created five or six lumpy "braids." To finish, she needed four or five times that many.

"You know what, sweetie?" Jo Lena said.

"We need to get you over to Lupe's house now so I can get busy on today's orders. Maybe you should leave the rest of her mane until tonight."

"Nope," Lily said, shaking her head. "She has to look pretty for Monte."

Jo Lena's heart sank through the floor again, for the thousandth time.

She tried to inject a light cheeriness into her voice.

"I — I'm thinking Monte may not be here to see her today, sugar."

Lily shrugged her shoulders.

"Never can tell," she said.

Suddenly, she turned around to look at Jo Lena.

"Let's pray about that," she said. "Tonight, can I go with you to the chapel?"

Jo Lena bit her lip and tried to think what to say.

Lord, please don't ever let her think that You've abandoned her, too, like Monte and her parents.

"You can go with me," Jo Lena said slowly, "but you must remember what we talked about the other day and pray for God's will to be done and not ours."

Lily nodded solemnly. "No problem," she said.

Jo Lena sighed. That expression was

something else she'd gotten from Monte.

Once he left the outskirts of Omaha, Monte took the two-lane highway that dropped straight south. Eventually, somewhere in Kansas, it'd lead him to I-35, and in the meantime it'd give him a quiet road, the dark countryside and tiny sleeping towns to help him think.

He was going home, but not to Jo Lena. He had to think about that. Jo Lena filled his mind; somewhere in the back of it he hadn't really stopped thinking about her since he left, and he had to get this straightened out with himself.

The Hill Country was where he belonged. He was going there because that was where he wanted to be. He did not want the responsibility of loving and being loved; therefore, he wasn't going back for Jo Lena.

He would stay away from her, emotionally. That was simple enough. If she agreed, they would be business partners in the bed-and-breakfast but nothing else. She was a fair person and she'd still let him be Lily Rae's "big brother" and her friend because she would understand that he couldn't deal with anything more.

She loved him. But she wouldn't always

love him. He had already disappointed her again, hadn't he? She probably thought he was gone for another six years.

Then his little voice of truth had to kick in.

Don't you think she could forgive you for leaving this time if she could forgive you for the past?

He also believed that she forgave him for Scotty and for leaving her in her grief. It had to be true because of the way she had put her arms around him for that kiss in her kitchen.

That one gesture, that sure and loving way that she had taken him into the fold of her embrace, had made him feel that all was well with Monte McMahan. That truth reverberated right through him, went right to the bone.

At last, at long, long last, he had actually felt that nothing was wrong with him.

Until that moment, it had been six long years since he had felt right. Probably he would never feel that way again.

Not if you stay away from her, you won't.

He had to stay away, though, so she'd not be telling him that God could forgive him, too. She was wrong about that.

His mouth opened and he spoke his thought into the empty cab.

"God," he said, "is Jo Lena right? Will You forgive me?"

Tears sprang to his eyes.

"I'm sorry, Lord," he said. "For everything. Will You please forgive me?"

The truck hummed on through the night, with the white and yellow lines flowing past it and the trees and fields looming dark and faraway in the torch of the headlights. Gradually, gently, Monte began to fill with the sense that Someone was with him.

It was nearing sundown when Monte drove up to the chapel in a cloud of white dust he'd raised from the gravel road. There were no vehicles anywhere around, but two horses waited patiently in the churchyard beneath a large mesquite tree.

He felt a quick clutch in his stomach. Someone was with Jo Lena? Before he left, her evening rides had been solitary and she'd visited the chapel alone.

Then, staring at the horses as he shut off the engine of the truck, he let his breath out in a long sigh. The long drive had eroded his eyesight. Or his mind. One of the horses carried a child-size saddle.

He got out of the truck and turned toward the chapel.

Two figures, hand in hand, one tall, one

tiny, stood in the open door, silhouetted by the red rays of the sun streaming in behind them. His heart gave a great thud.

He wished for words, he wished for more time.

He wished he had come back sooner.

Monte swung around, reached into the back seat and picked up the hat. Then he started up the walk, stretching his stiff legs that grew longer and quicker with each stride. He needed to see Jo's face. He needed to touch her.

They were awfully quiet, completely still. Were they both mad at him? Lily Rae wasn't even running to meet him.

She *was* talking to him, though.

"Monte," she said, "is that my hat?"

"I bought it for you, Lil," he said, grinning down at her as he reached them, "but now I'm thinking it may be a better fit for your mama instead."

He glanced from her blond head to Jo Lena's as if judging the size.

Jo Lena's stance was wary, but she seemed to be smiling at the hat. Then he thought she smiled at him, but since she was still in the shadows he couldn't be certain.

"N-o-o," Lily said, giggling, "it fits *me* instead."

He fit the hat onto her shiny hair.

"I don't know," he said, teasing her. "It looks a little big."

Lily Rae wasn't worried at all.

"It's mine," she said, pulling it down more firmly. "Now, what did you bring my mama?"

"Lily Rae, remember your manners," Jo Lena said in her sweet, husky voice.

Only then did he find the courage to look directly at her.

She definitely was smiling at him now. That was a good sign.

His eyes held hers. They'd lost a week in the present and six years in the past. That was enough time to waste.

Dear God, let her say that she'll have me.

"My heart," he said, still looking at Jo Lena. "For your mama, I brought my dusty old heart."

"Good," Lily Rae said. "She'll like that."

Then she pirouetted happily out onto the low, flat steps of the church and onto the walk, calling to the horses about her new hat.

Monte heard her, but he didn't see her. He couldn't see anything but Jo Lena.

"Is Lil right?" he said. "Do you like it that I brought you my heart?"

He reached out and took her hand, pulled her out into the low-slanting sunlight.

"I'd like to like it," she said, "but I need to know how you got from 'Don't love me' to 'Here's my heart, hope you like it.' "

She pulled her hand free and walked on past him to sit down on the low wall that ran along the flagstone path. He followed.

"God," he said. "He picked me up and moved me from one place to the other."

He sat down beside her.

"Don't you believe me, Jo?"

Her eyes were filling with tears.

"You're the one who said it," he said. "God gave me to you to love, Jo Lena, and you can't go back on that now."

She laughed and touched his face.

"This has been the most incredible day," she said. "I'll never forget it if I live to be a hundred years old."

His heart swelled.

"I'll never forget you said that, Jo Lena."

That made her laugh again.

"It's not all because of you, Monte," she said.

He pretended great disappointment, and to tell the truth, he was a little bit worried. Had that light in her eyes been there before he ever arrived? Was it not all for him?

"Did somebody else give you a heart, too?"

"No. A child. My child. Your friend Ned

is a master negotiator."

A huge relief flowed through him and he forgot to be jealous.

"So it's definite? You have total custody?"

"They started drawing up the papers today."

"Good old Ned," he said.

Satisfaction pumped him up. He, Monte, *had* done something good for her, after all.

He took both her hands in his.

"I'm thinking it's not too late to get the names changed on those papers," he said.

She searched his eyes as if she were looking for his very soul.

"Changed to what?"

"McMahan," he said. "Mr. and Mrs. Monte."

She narrowed her eyes at him and pretended to think about that.

"Hmm," she said.

But her fingers were clinging to his for dear life.

"We've already burned way too much daylight, Jo Lena, and you know it," he said. "You have thirty seconds to give me your answer."

"What if it's 'no'?" she said.

"Then you have the rest of your life to change your mind. I'm here to stay this time."

"Thank goodness," she said as she lifted her face to his, "because if you ever left me again, I'd have to follow you . . ."

Monte kissed the rest of the words away. They didn't need them anyway.

Epilogue

Bobbie Ann sat back on her heels with her trowel in her hand and feasted her eyes on her children and grandchildren. Never, ever, even a year ago, would she have dreamed of such riches.

"Let's put that variegated moss all along the west wall of the chapel," Cait called to Monte and Clint, who were unloading flats of spring flowers and plants from the back of the truck.

She shifted baby Clint IV — generally called Rowdy because he truly was — to a more comfortable spot on her hip, gave him an absentminded kiss on the head and added, "That moss blooms in the sun and I want to see the flowers."

Rowdy bucked in her arms, wanting down, but she paid him no mind. LydaAnn and Delia, doting aunts, were unfolding his blankets and spreading them out on top of a saddle pad. Lily Rae was earnestly helping them.

Cait the horsewoman was becoming quite

the mother and quite the gardener, too. She was making lots of things grow on the Rocking M in addition to that mustard seed of faith she'd planted in Clint's heart.

New flower beds for the chapel had been her idea and getting all the family to plant them had been Bobbie Ann's. Sometimes she just needed to get every one of them together so she could watch them and listen to them and feel them all around her.

"Can you see the flowers from your house, Cait?" Darcy called.

"I'm thinking we'll be able to," Cait said. "We're pretty high up on the hill."

Clint and Cait had built a new house on the ranch and so had Monte and Jo Lena, who had found living at the busiest bed-and-breakfast in Texas way too public and hectic for newlyweds. Very different houses, yet they both had the same old-Texas limestone ranch house looks as the main house.

"We'll enjoy them every time we drive by," Darcy said, chasing after three-year-old Maegan who was on her way to disciplining her one-year-old brother, Michael, for toddling around picking the pretty flowers. "All of the chapel we can see from our house is the cross and the bell tower."

Darcy and Jackson had been too attached to Old Clint's house to move from there, so they'd renovated and built an addition on to it. Bobbie Ann smiled. They were talking about having more children, so they might have to do yet another addition to the old place.

She looked at Jackson, whistling while he worked at setting up the folding table for Jo Lena to put out the food. Thank the Lord for sending His Good Samaritan, Darcy, to help Jackson recover from that terrible funk he'd been in for so long.

"We can see the cross from our house, too," Jo Lena said. "I was surprised, since we're farther away."

Bobbie Ann watched Jo Lena's contented smile as she started across the churchyard. Jo Lena was looking around and counting her blessings, too, including Monte, the prodigal son, who had come home at last and stayed because of her.

And she was bringing so much food out of her vehicle that it could hardly all fit on the table.

"Jo Lena, the next time we get together I'll do the cooking," Bobbie Ann called to her. "You'll have your hands full with the twins."

Jo Lena glanced down at her enormous belly.

"You know, Bobbie Ann," she said. "I

think I'll take you up on that. Now all I have to do is find a good assistant manager for the bed-and-breakfast, and I'll be all set to take care of these two little cowboys."

"Oh, Jo Lena, I forgot to tell you what Hank said," Delia said. "He thinks since the name Rowdy is already taken, you should call your boys Bronc and Buster."

Everybody laughed and Delia beamed as if Hank were the cleverest man on earth.

"Why didn't you ask Hank to come over and help us today, Delia?" Bobbie Ann said.

Delia scowled.

"Oh, Mom. We've only had two dates. Now don't start one of your campaigns of trying to get me married off."

"I wouldn't think of it."

But Delia was blushing. She was pretty interested in Hank.

Bobbie Ann smiled to herself as she began turning up the earth for the yucca plants. In her opinion, Delia and LydaAnn both needed to find good husbands to complete their busy lives. Maybe there'd be *lots* more grandchildren one of these days.

Maybe God would bless her with as many grandchildren as there were flowers around the old chapel.

About the Author

GENA DALTON wanted to be a professional writer since she learned to read at the age of four. However, she became a secondary school teacher and then a college professor/dean of women instead, and began to write after she was married and a stay-at-home mother. She entered an essay contest that resulted in a newspaper publication, giving her confidence she could achieve her lifelong dream of becoming a "real writer."

Gena lives in Oklahoma with her husband of twenty-four years. Now that their son is grown, their only companions are two dogs, two house cats, one barn cat and one cat who belongs to the neighbors but won't go home.

She loves to hear from readers. She can be reached c/o Steeple Hill Books, 300 East 42nd Street, New York, NY 10017.

Dear Reader,

This story of Monte, the third McMahan brother and Bobbie Ann's prodigal son, is one we can all relate to from our own experience. Who among us hasn't felt separated from those we love by our choices and actions? At those times when we are farthest away, we all long to go home.

Monte takes the long way home, for he not only has stayed away for six years while rarely communicating with his mother, brothers and sisters, but he has also denied his yearning to see Jo Lena Speirs, the only woman he has ever loved. He believes he is past redemption, in God's eyes and in Jo Lena's, because of the death of her brother, Scotty. He bears a burning guilt that he has not been able to escape, even by traveling thousands of miles and putting himself in constant danger.

From the instant that Monte gets thrown from a bull and is hurt too badly to ride, he knows that he can no longer bear to be so alone. He sneaks onto the Rocking M, and dreads seeing anyone there, especially Jo Lena, but from the moment he arrives on the ranch, he knows that at last he has come home.

If you haven't read the stories of Monte's brothers, Jackson and Clint, please look for

Stranger at the Crossroads and *Midnight Faith*, both also published by Steeple Hill. I would love to hear from you. You can reach me c/o Steeple Hill Books, 300 East 42nd Street, New York, NY 10017.

All warm wishes,

Gena Dalton